PRAISE FOR *MY SO-CALLED SUPERPOWERS*

"*My So-Called Superpowers* is vibrant, lively, and hums along at a snappy pace. It has a **genuinely warm**, welcoming Saturday-morning cartoon feeling to it."
—Tony Cliff, *New York Times*–bestselling author of the Delilah Dirk series

"A **hilarious** tale of a girl so desperate to be cool that she defies her best judgment to get what she wants."
—*Bulletin of the Center for Children's Books*

"Heather Nuhfer has hilariously and achingly captured what it's like to be in middle school, trying to control the weird things that make you different but also super. And it's impossible not to root for Veronica. **Super real, super fun, and just generally and genuinely super.**"
—Dana Simpson, author of the Phoebe and Her Unicorn series

"Readers will be delighted at Veronica's relatable quirkiness . . . a **whimsical, good-humored**, straightforward take on just loving yourself for who you are."
—*Booklist*

Also by Heather Nuhfer

My So-Called Superpowers

My So-Called SUPERPOWERS

MY SO-CALLED SUPERPOWERS

MIXED EMOTIONS

HEATHER NUHFER

ILLUSTRATIONS BY SIMINI BLOCKER

[Imprint]
MAKE YOUR MARK

New York

{Imprint}
MAKE YOUR MARK

A part of Macmillan Publishing Group, LLC
175 Fifth Avenue, New York, NY 10010

Library of Congress Control Number: 2018944986

ISBN 978-1-250-13862-0 (hardcover) / ISBN 978-1-250-13861-3 (ebook)

Our books may be purchased in bulk for promotional, educational, or business use.
Please contact your local bookseller or the Macmillan Corporate and Premium
Sales Department at (800) 221-7945 ext. 5442 or by email at
MacmillanSpecialMarkets@macmillan.com.

Book design by Ellen Duda

Imprint logo designed by Amanda Spielman

First edition, 2019

1 3 5 7 9 10 8 6 4 2

mackids.com

If illegally download this book you must,
forever more your farts shall combust.

For my parents, Tom and Dolly Nuhfer, who inspire me to stay curious

CHAPTER ONE
THERE AND BACK AGAIN: A WEIRDO'S TALE

So, here we are again. At last. For the first time.

Confused? Yep. Me, too. Let's work on this together, shall we? Last time we talked I had this whole . . . thing going on. Well, news flash: I still do. Some people (my best friend, Charlie) insist on calling this thing "superpowers," but to me, the honorable Veronica McGowan, superpowers are for the truly super among us: guys with capes and ladies with lassos. Not twelve-year-old me.

Also important: Those Super People have control of when and how their powers pop up. Their powers are something they intentionally use for good. And, believe me, <u>intentionally</u> is the underlined word here.

No, I definitely would not use the word super *to describe what comes outta me. "Stupid" seems to fit the bill. At least in my mind. Stupidpowers.*

Know it.

Live it.

Love it?

I'm gonna take a hard pass on that last one.

Don't get me wrong. I've come full circle on my powers. I've learned to more or less accept that they're a part of me. An embarrassing, endlessly annoying part of me. I still hide them and I still think I'd be better off without them, to be honest, but who wouldn't wish to be stupidpower-free if whenever you were surprised, your head could literally pop off? I think I'm being fair with myself.

"Excuse me?"

Abruptly removed from my inner monologue, I looked up to see the weary, unsmiling face of my dad's 3:45 p.m. dental appointment.

"Off in your own little world, there?" the woman in front of me asked.

I nodded and opened the schedule on the computer. "Sorry about that. Ms. Milner, right?"

"I am. And you shouldn't be sorry. It's a beautiful day. Who wants to spend it at the dentist? Not me."

"Maybe we should both make a break for it," I joked.

I couldn't have agreed with Ms. Milner more. Summer was here, school was still four whole beautiful weeks away, and I was paying off my debt to society (meaning, in this case, my dad, Rik) by working at his dental practice three days a week. Despite my printing out many documents on child labor laws and sticking them to the fridge, Dad hadn't budged on his punishment for when I snuck a few underage kids into the nightclub he also works at. But I had learned my lesson. Did we really need to keep this shame show going? Case in point: Actual conversation I recently had when I bumped into Kate from school at the grocery store:

"Hi, Kate! How's your summer going?"

"Pretty good. I've been taking waterskiing lessons at the lake, you know, and reading some books. Pretty boring. You?"

"Uh, well, I've learned how to organize forms for the insurance biller and can now replace those long overhead light bulbs."

Ms. Milner forced a polite cough, bringing me back to reality.

"I did it again, didn't I?" I said. "Sorry. Have a seat."
As a joke, I tapped my fingertips together menacingly and
added, in my spookiest voice, "The doctor will see you
shortly. Bwa-ha-ha!"

Ms. Milner pulled an uneasy smile.

Humor. It's not for everyone.

I heard dad's deep voice bellow down the hall as he
brought his previous patient, Mr. Rutledge, back out to the
waiting room.

"Who doesn't love a good caramel?" Dad asked.

"That's exactly what I'm saying!" Mr. Rutledge replied.

"Next time, more adhesive, or just gum it," Dad advised.

Mr. Rutledge winked at Dad as he put his baseball cap
over his silver hair. "Will do, Doc!"

Dad shook his hand. "My best to Maggie, okay?"

"Of course, of course." Mr. Rutledge gave me a wide
smile. "You two behave!" His dentures looked much
better—and certainly less caramel encrusted—than when
he'd come in.

"I'll try to keep him in line," I joked back.

"Have a lovely weekend!" Mr. Rutledge waved on his
way out the door.

"Veri, Ms. Milner's file plea—" Dad stopped, staring

at the state of the reception desk. He gave me "the look." You know the look. The "Really? We have to talk about this *again*?" look.

"Sorry," I mumbled and then fumbled through the stacks of files I was supposed to put back yesterday and the day before. After a valiant recovery mission, I unearthed Ms. Milner's file from under my current sketching project, which also happened to be spread across the desk. The overturned pencil case, about thirty half-full water glasses, and open comic books probably didn't help the overall look of things, either.

"I'm really bad at this," I said, handing over the file.

"Yep." He tried not to smile.

"Encouragement might help, Father dearest." I playfully smacked his arm and we laughed.

"Lost cause, kiddo. Clean it up, then you can go home. And don't burn the place down," he instructed as he led Ms. Milner down the hall.

I wasn't entirely sure if he was kidding. Probably? I wasn't angry, so the likelihood of me breathing fire was pretty slim. Now that Dad knew about my powers, and I knew that he also had powers, things had been a lot easier between us. I hated keeping such a giant secret from him.

Obviously, I'll always have some tiny secrets, but hopefully not any more huge, gym-wrecking ones like I used to have. Hmm. Let me sum up. It had been a pretty intense school year: My stupidpowers started happening, basically ruining my life. My friend Charlie had done his best to help out, but there wasn't much he could do. I'd been sure my long-lost mother had given the powers to me, and I'd kept the whole thing secret from Dad. Finally, so many people knew about my weird abilities, and so many terrible, embarrassing things had really gotten to me, that I kind of turned into a human tornado of disaster. But somehow it all worked out—and nearly everyone's memory of what happened was wiped. Of course, the school gym did get destroyed, but as long as no one knew it was my fault . . . I mean, they can build another gym. I only have the one life, though. And I found out that my dad had powers, too! So did my great grandma Beatrice!

The biggest bummer was that his powers were so different from mine, he isn't that much of a help. His ability to heal fast and help other people heal fast was far more super than anything that ever came out of me. Over the years his powers have gotten weaker and don't seem to cause him any grief whatsoever. It's great to have someone who understands just how weird it all is, but in terms of management or curing this mess, we are both clueless.

I was halfway through the tower of manila files when Charlie rushed in. His red hair was plastered back from sweat. He must have run the whole way to the office! His gigantic smile told me he was really excited about something.

"Veri! Veri!" Charlie wheezed, leaning over to catch his breath. He reached toward one of the water glasses on my desk. "Water," he gasped dramatically.

"Don't drink that!" I warned him. "I don't know how long it's been there. Or if it's even water." I filled a fresh paper cup from the water cooler and handed it to him. "What is it?"

He chugged the whole thing before exclaiming, "Film Camp!" He crushed the paper cup triumphantly, then fished a sweat-dampened leaflet out of his back pocket and offered it to me.

I gingerly took it, using only the nails of my index finger and thumb.

"Sorry 'bout that," he said. "It's really hot out there."

"It's okay. I mean, it's just sweat. Butt sweat. *Your* butt sweat."

He snatched the pamphlet back. "Why don't I just hold it?"

"Good idea!"

Charlie opened the once-glossy advertisement for a new local day camp for eight- to thirteen-year-olds who are interested in film and television production.

"This. Looks. Amazing!" I gushed, seeing all the pictures of other kids behind real cameras and clapping those little chalkboard things while yelling *Action!* I've always wanted to yell *Action!*

Charlie was just as excited. "You could learn more about storyboarding and production design! And I could become a world-famous actor!"

"Holy moly!" I could feel my excitement going into the danger zone, but it was too late—my powers switched on, and miniature fireworks burst around us.

Charlie and I had always loved movies, but since school let out we'd become obsessed. Partly because I was still struggling with my powers and wanted to keep a low profile, but also because it had been so freaking hot and there aren't many places two twelve-year-olds can just hang out. We'd had one ill-fated trip to the public pool when someone did not respect the funny sign that read THIS IS OUR

OOL. NOTICE THERE IS NO P IN IT. WE'D LIKE TO KEEP IT THAT WAY. There wasn't enough chlorine in the world to get Charlie and me back in that pool.

Air-conditioning had become the only salvation. The old theater downtown had classic movies on the weekend. And during the week, on my days off, we took the bus into Jamestown, the next city over, where they have a proper modern movie theater to see new movies. It didn't matter what was playing. We'd see it all! And every single cent of our allowance went to it. In fact, this weekend we were planning on going to a horror film fest at the old movie theater.

"Whoa! Camp starts on Monday?" I asked, skimming the important info.

"That's the mad thing," Charlie explained. "It's my brother Nick—he's running it for part of his college credit!"

"Oh, no way!"

I'd always liked Nick. He was consistently nice to me and mostly nice to Charlie, but I guess not being 100 percent there is common among brothers. Anyway, I was sad when he left for college last year.

"We gotta do this," I said, but as soon as the words were out of my mouth, I remembered where I was and who I was beholden to. "Oh, crud."

Charlie helped me file the rest of my mess and get the reception area back in order. Then we waited. I was grateful that Charlie was staying to give me moral support. Plus, my dad really liked him. You could tell by how much he teased Charlie. I was hoping that might help grease the wheels of the camp train.

"Hey, chief!" Dad greeted Charlie as he waved goodbye to Ms. Milner. She had a little drool dripping from the corner of her mouth. She must've still been numb.

"How goes it, Rik?" Charlie asked.

"Fan-freaking-Friday-tastic, my friend," he answered, then he frowned. "What are you guys still doing here?" he asked, a bit more suspiciously than I would have liked.

"I have something to ask you," I said, nodding to Charlie to hand over the camp pamphlet.

Charlie furrowed his brow and looked at me. "But you said it had bu—"

"It's fine!" I cut him off. "It's fine."

Charlie shrugged and handed it to Dad, who read it over, looking up at us occasionally.

I swallowed hard. "I know that I am supposed to be working here all summer, but this is only for two weeks. And I think it will be a really good learning experience, so

11

it won't just be like I'm off having fun. I'll have to learn things. And be good. And you'll know where I am all the time." I was rambling now, but I couldn't stop. "And Charlie's brother is running it—he's been at film school for a whole year! So, you can even ask him about it. And he can tell you how well behaved I'm being."

"Yeah," Charlie added, "he definitely won't let us have very much fun."

Dad handed back the sweaty pamphlet and then spun the ring on his right hand around and around. This was a sure sign he was thinking about it. I could hear my heart beating in my chest. It was getting louder and faster the more nervous and excited I got. Both Dad and Charlie looked at me. Then Charlie plugged his ears.

"Oh, can you guys hear that, too?" I asked, but immediately had to repeat myself much louder. My powers were making my heartbeat unbelievably loud. "Sorry, I'm just a little excited." Charlie patted me on the back and I took a few deep breaths. Finally, the volume on my ticker went down enough so we could talk.

"Well," Dad said, "to afford it, we'd have to be pretty thrifty the rest of the summer. You understand that?"

"Yes!" Charlie and I said in unison.

"That means BYO Creamsicles, Charlie."

"I'm cool with that!" Charlie, the master destroyer of Creamsicles, replied.

"And no movies beyond the classic theater. It's too expensive at that megaplex dump."

"Understood," I said as seriously as I could. "We'll be *making* the movies we want to see."

"Okay." Dad nodded, a smile curling his lips. "Have fun."

Charlie and I looked at each other, mouths wide open for a solid ten seconds before the happy shouts followed. We went to hug, but then fell short. That was a new thing of weirdness. So instead I turned and gave Dad the biggest hug I could.

"Thank you! Thank you so much!" I yelled, giving him an extra squeeze on each word.

"Watch the eardrums!" he said, and laughed. "And honestly, I wanted to fire you anyway. You really are the absolute worst at this."

"Yeah. Can't blame you there," I agreed as I stopped smooshing him. "But who will you get to take my place?"

"I have an idea," he said as we locked up, "but I'm pretty sure you're gonna hate it."

CHAPTER TWO
CAMP...WHATEVER

Dad was right. He was so, so very right. And the proof is sitting next to me at a now-immaculate reception desk.

"I'm not exactly sure why you are here, McGowan," Ms. Watson said plainly as she spritzed a small fern on her desk with water. She had brought the fern with her.

I'd thought Ms. Watson was just the new guidance counselor at school last year. Then it turned out she was a government agent who'd been investigating the superpowers in my family for years. True story: Her name wasn't even Watson. It was Hendriks! I still called her Ms. Watson. Everyone did, and she didn't seem to mind. Anyway, somehow Dad and I convinced her not to turn us in—and she'd also gotten fired from her job, so I guess she was now . . . harmless? That didn't mean I wanted her to take over my old job in Dad's office, though.

"Dad said I needed to orientate you before I went to camp," I told her.

"So tell me what you know," she demanded, focusing every ounce of attention on me.

"I know nothing!" I squealed. "I mean, you obviously got this."

"Basic office work," she agreed, tapping a razor-sharp pencil on a notepad. "Now that I'm a full-time guidance counselor and no longer a government agent, I have to do the same thing as most other brave folks literally molding the lives of the future leaders of our great country: I have to get a second job." She broke the pencil in half.

"Well, at least you don't have to worry about keeping incredible government secrets anymore, right?" I offered.

"True. Now it's just *your* incredible secrets."

The joke was so unexpected that I snorted. "Ms. Watson, you made a joke!"

"I've read that levity can ease social situations."

Just then, Dad came back from his run to the coffee shop.

"Doughnuts!" I gasped with delight. "I thought we were watching our dough and not buying doughnuts."

"Well, it's Isabella's first day," he said.

"Doughnuts are traditional for that," I agreed. Wait. "Isabella?" I waited for Ms. Watson to correct him or staple his lips together or something. She didn't.

I decided not to think about it any further. "I gotta go," I said. I had greatness to chase!

"Good luck, Veri!" Dad said, his mouth full of jelly-filled miracle.

Ms. Watson added, "Break a leg."

I grabbed a doughnut and ran. My future in film awaited me.

Camp was being held at the little local theater, which currently housed summer stock. They had a nighttime production that ran from Friday through Sunday, but they were going to let the film camp use the stage and the large park next to the building during the day. I had tried out for their current production of *Peter Pan*, but I didn't get the part. Truthfully, I had made a big fool of myself in the process, and that was before I even knew I had powers. I could only imagine what a disaster it would be if I were in that production now. Trying to hide my powers while onstage?! It would be terrifying.

Charlie and I had spent the weekend at the classic theater's Horror Fest. We had been really excited for it, but after learning we were going to camp, the movies took on a whole new level of importance. Notes were taken. Opinions were formed. Nightmares were had.

The theater was just a short walk from Dad's office, and I knew Charlie would be there already, since he was getting a ride with Nick. I was a little scared about what my powers might do in the next two weeks, but at least I could hide among all the other campers—unlike the Weathers brothers, who stuck out no matter where they were. I spotted them by their bright red hair long before I could make out their faces.

Just outside the theater entrance, Charlie was helping Nick set up a table for the campers to check in at.

"Hey, Veronica!" Nick greeted me with a big smile. He'd grown his hair out to just above his shoulders. He had managed some stubble, too, which made him look a lot older than the last time I'd seen him. Nick was one of those super-genius kids and had skipped two grades when he was younger than Charlie and me. He was only eighteen, but he'd been away at film school in New York for over a year. Their parents, well, one of their parents, was really unhappy Nick was "wasting" his brain at film school, but he was doing it anyway. It was ridiculously cool.

"Nick! Uh, hi! How are you?" I asked.

"Great, great. Just back from school a couple days ago." He handed me my name tag. "This should be fun, right?"

"Totally fun," I reassured him.

"I've told him that a million times just this morning, so don't expect him to listen," Charlie chimed in. "I think he's nervous."

"I get it," I said. "I would be, too. I mean, what kind of college manly man wants to spend two weeks with a bunch of kids, amiright?" I gave Nick a gentle bro punch on his shoulder.

Nick chuckled. "It's just a lot of preparation. I'm worried I forgot something."

"Don't worry. Charlie and I can help." I got to work sorting through the name tags. Besides me and Charlie, there were only six other kids registered for camp. So much for me hiding in a crowd.

"Don't worry about it, Veronica," Nick said, waving me away. "The reinforcements have arrived. Meet your camp counselors!"

I looked up and saw Ted, our favorite pretzel-serving guru at the local mall—always giving me and Charlie odd advice at odd moments, but in a friendly way—and a girl who works at the classic movie theater. Guessing from the name tag options, I figured her name was Ellie. She was constantly changing the color of her waist-length hair. Today it was a shiny swath of periwinkle blue. She had also braided a chunk of it and wrapped it over the top of her head like a headband. She looked like a mermaid, and I was really jealous. For whatever dumb reason, Dad had decided I can't actually dye my hair until I'm sixteen, so I was stuck using wash-out dyes that barely show up on my chestnut brown hair.

I was thinking about Ellie's hair for so long that I missed the entirety of everyone saying hello to each other. This is where I came back to Earth:

"So, wait, wait, wait." Ted leaned back against the table and scratched his head. "You two are brothers? Biologically?

I always assumed you didn't grow up together, 'cause, you know, Charlie's accent."

"We aren't British," Nick answered matter-of-factly.

"Mum is," Charlie reminded him.

Nick ruffled Charlie's hair. "And we are adopted."

Charlie nodded casually, like talking with a fake British accent was a normal thing that lots of people did in their everyday lives. To him, it was no big deal. I admired Charlie for that. Not surprisingly, Ted thought it was pretty cool, too.

"All right, little man. You be you!" Ted high-fived Charlie.

Ellie added, "It threw me off, too. You guys have been coming to the movies so much this summer. I wish I had known you were Nick's brother."

"Yeah," Nick chimed in. "Ellie and I graduated together."

"But you're not at college yet?" I asked.

"No." Ellie turned a little red with embarrassment. "I'm saving up money. Hopefully I can go next semester."

"Cool," I said. I felt bad that I had embarrassed her, and I wanted to give her time to recover. So, naturally, I started rambling. "I'm Veronica, by the way. I'm Charlie's best friend. We've been best friends our whole lives, pretty much. We're in middle school, but I bet we will still be best friends when we're in high school. Like you and Nick were. I mean, not that you were best friends, but friends. In high school. Like Charlie and I will be."

Nick shot Charlie a questioning look and Charlie shrugged his reply.

I was still trying to smooth things over with Ellie. "And I love your hair."

This made her blush again, but luckily, we were both spared further humiliation. Campers were starting to wander in. I knew the faces of most of them but not the names. A lot of them were younger than Charlie and me. Then I spotted a very familiar face and flinched. A quick spark of fear sent a short wave of my powers through me. I watched one of my fluffy curls turn white. I quickly tucked it behind my ear and out of sight.

It was Betsy.

She used to be my nemesis, but things had been better with Betsy since the whole gym-destroying incident. She had been spared the mind wipe everyone else had gotten to make them forget about my powers, but she still hadn't spilled the beans to anyone about my condition. Nor had she attempted to murder me or otherwise ruin my life, which was a daily goal for her last year at school. I wasn't sure if she liked me now or if she was terrified of me. Either way, I didn't want to disturb the uneasy peace of the past few months.

"You okay?" Charlie whispered to me after spotting Betsy.

"Maybe if we just don't make eye contact?" I whispered back. "You know, just completely ignore each other for the next two weeks?"

"I endorse this plan," Charlie said.

Betsy greeted us as she walked by. "Charlie. Weirdo."

"Hi?" Charlie squeaked out. I was unable to move.

After Betsy was inside, I looked at Charlie. "She said hi?! What was that?!"

Charlie raised an eyebrow. "A sign of the apocalypse, for sure."

Once all the campers had checked in, Charlie and I followed the counselors into the theater. It was tiny but pristine. As one of the only historical sites in Pearce, our small town, it stayed well maintained and was a rather fancy place. There was no movie screen; only a stage for plays and speakers and all manner of fancy entertainment. Until this summer, only the summer stock *thespian* (a fancy word for an actor in plays) people got to use it, so I had never been backstage, and when Dad and I saw a show we never sat anywhere near the front of the theater. He isn't that fond of crowds. Or musical numbers. Anyway, I was excited to plop myself down in one of the blue velvet seats and learn the craft of filmmaking. But first, I guess, we had to do the boring stuff.

"Introductions," Nick said after he, Ellie, and Ted took the stage and told us about themselves. "Charlie, why don't you break the ice? Tell us who you are and what you're most eager to learn about."

Charlie was happy to oblige and stood up so everyone could see him. "I'm Charlie Weathers. Yes, Nick is my older, less handsome brother. I'm interested mainly in acting."

Next, two kids stood up simultaneously. I recognized them from school—Lizzie and Dean. They were twins and in the Tech Club, which gained them the glorious nickname, "the Tech Twins." It wasn't just the tech that made them so notable. They weren't identical at all, but both had large birthmarks on their forearms. When they stood close enough together that their arms touched, the birthmarks matched up and made a heart shape. I'm not even kidding. It was the coolest!

I tried to get into the Tech Club last year, but I bailed after I unknowingly set a magnet on top of something called "floppy disks," which I guess used to be how you saved stuff on old computers. Turns out the magnet erased all the info on the discs. Moral of the story: Technology used to be really delicate.

Anyway, they introduced themselves and—spoiler alert—they wanted to learn all things tech at camp.

Betsy kept it short and simple. "Betsy. I want to improve my cinematography skills here. At Camp . . . whatever."

Then there was a trio of kids who I had seen at school, but never met. I think they were nine or ten. Whenever I saw them they were huddled together playing that card game Magic: The Gathering. The only way to really differentiate them was their height: small one, tall one, and super-tall one. But now it seemed like Rashida, at least, wanted everyone to see her. And talk to her. Possibly all at once. She was interested in advertising, social media campaigns, and stuff like that and was often texting on one phone while talking on another. It was a skill I deeply admired. She wanted to learn about "getting the buzz out." There was also Max, who was all about costumes. He told us that he was way into LARPing and going, in costume, to renaissance fairs. He wore a different style hat every day to fit his mood. Today he was wearing a sea captain's cap. Then we got to Avery, who stood but was dead silent for way too long.

"Anytime you're ready, pal," Nick encouraged him.

Finally, Rashida took pity on him. "This is Avery and he is an actor."

Avery still said nothing as he removed his thick black-framed glasses and cleaned them with the hem of his T-shirt.

Charlie leaned in and whispered in my ear, "Silent film star?"

Then it was my turn.

"Hey, I'm Veronica McGowan." My voice quivered a bit, so I coughed to make it look like I just had something stuck in my throat. "I'm, um, really curious about story-boarding and production design. I, uh, I like to draw."

I quickly sat down, gloriously relieved that nothing embarrassing had happened.

Then Nick and Ellie sat on the edge of the stage and started telling us all about their plans for the next two weeks of camp. It became very obvious that Ellie was just as excited about this camp as Nick was. She explained that she was helping Nick run the camp and that we should feel free to come to her if we needed anything. Their plan was pretty simple and amazing! We were going to make a movie! We would write it, act it, film it, edit it—everything! Along the way, we'd each focus on what we wanted to learn most and our counselors would teach us everything they knew. Next Friday, on the last day of camp, we would have a premiere for our friends and family at the Weatherses' house. I couldn't believe we could really make a movie in less than two weeks! It was super exciting!

"So, the first thing to decide is what our film is going to be about. We need a story," Nick said.

"What genre?" Charlie asked.

Ellie answered, "What genre—or what type—of film is totally up to you. Drama, comedy, superhero, take your pick."

"Horror?" I wondered aloud, thinking about the past weekend.

"Yes!" Charlie practically bounced out of his seat.

Some of the other kids sounded like they agreed with Charlie.

Nick smiled at me, but he seemed a little surprised at my suggestion. "What type of horror were you thinking, Veronica?"

"*Umm.*" I fumbled a bit. Everyone was looking at me. "I, uh, was thinking about classic horror. Like the ones from the 1970s."

"So, not like black-and-white, cheesy 1950s monster movies?" Nick asked.

"You're thinking more like the ones we had at the movie theater for our Horror Movie Festival, like *Jaws*, or *Westworld*?" Ellie chimed in. I was eternally grateful.

"Uh, yeah. Yeah! I think it would be cool to have a monster, though." My brain finally caught up to the possibilities of what we could do and started to focus less on the stares.

"Yes! I want to make a monster costume!" Max loudly agreed.

No one else said anything. I panicked—and worried my powers might start doing their thing.

"It's a horror movie," I said, "so it doesn't have to be that long, and we won't need a ton of resources, so I think it might be a good fit for a first movie. Did that make any sense?"

"That is"—Nick paused—"pretty brilliant. What do you guys think?"

"Such an awesome idea, Veri!" Charlie agreed.

The other kids were now talking excitedly among themselves. They liked the idea!

"I think we have a winner," Nick said. He sounded proud.

The mix of shyness and unexpected success made my cheeks get warm, and I could definitely feel something stirring inside. I'd started to notice that sometimes before my powers hit, I'd get this sort of fluttery feeling in my stomach. Not a good feeling, like when you see your crush—more like when you just ate a huge plate of nachos and then rode a roller coaster five times in a row.

"Yeah, whatever," Betsy grumbled, and put her feet on the seat in front of her.

"That's the spirit, Betsy," Nick said, and winked at me.

And that did me in. I could feel my powers ramping up, and it just made me want to disappear.

"I gotta go, Charlie," I whispered.

"Why?" he whispered back.

I was trying to climb over him, but it wasn't going so well. It seemed like every two days Charlie had an extra three inches of leg. I could tell my powers were about to become very public, so I slid on my belly over the next seat. The toe of my sneaker caught Betsy in the ear.

"Hey!" She swatted at my foot.

"So sorry!" I reached out to her, but then I noticed my hand was starting to disappear. I kept sliding out to the aisle and backed away out the door.

Safely in the lobby, I took a few deep breaths. I wasn't actually sure if the breathing helped calm down the powers, but it couldn't hurt.

Charlie tiptoed out into the lobby, quietly closing the auditorium door behind him.

"Powers?" he asked.

I rolled my eyes and showed him that three of my fingers were still invisible.

"What is it from this time?" he asked.

"A mix of things, I guess," I said. I didn't want to tell him *everything*. "Are they freaked out?"

"Nah, I told them you were stung by a bee," he said.

I giggled. "Thanks for that."

"'Tis my duty," Charlie said. "I think we're all supposed to head outside and brainstorm our plot."

As if on cue, the rest of the campers came out of the

auditorium. I gave Charlie a look and stuffed my missing fingers into my pocket. Ellie crouched down next to me.

"Are you okay? You're not allergic, right?" she asked.

"Nope," I said. "I'm okay. I don't even think I was stung. Maybe just bit by a bug."

"Like a deadly fire ant!" Charlie said.

Ellie's eyes went big as moons.

"Or something simple and not terrifying," I reassured her. "Like a mosquito."

Charlie grinned. "Maybe one carrying the West Nile virus?"

I swear Ellie's face turned white as a ghost. Charlie really needed to stop being "helpful."

"Or," I declared, looking right at Charlie, "I'm totally fine and we don't need to talk about it anymore."

Charlie, realizing he was making things worse, pulled himself out of his death-by-bugs spiral. "Oh! Yeah, no. Ellie, she is fine. Probably a flea. I bet her dog has fleas."

I gave up.

When Ellie, Charlie, and I joined the rest of the campers, Nick had already written a few ideas on a giant pad of paper he had set up on a stand.

"Well . . . ," Nick said, "we have one of the most classic issues for young, independent filmmakers: We have no budget. So we need to look around at what we do have and find a way to build our story around that. Using real locations and props will add realism and create production value—"

Ellie joined him, adding, "Which is essentially anything that makes your film look, sound, or feel better to the audience."

"Yes. If we can use our actual surroundings and the things we have, our film will be all the better for it. Thanks, El." Nick patted her elbow awkwardly.

"Well, we have the lake," Charlie piped up, "and we can make a monster, so why not a lake monster?"

"Yeah," I agreed, "and it could be an old-school, like, scary monster who has been imprisoned beneath the lake for years and years and years and is woken up."

"Accidentally woken up," Betsy added. "It's always an accident."

Lizzie raised her birthmarked arm to get our attention. "We could do some underwater lighting to make it look like he has broken through from another world!"

"That sounds awesome!" Ellie said.

"But the costume shouldn't go in the water," Max informed us as he adjusted his captain's hat. "It'll mess it all up."

"We can work around that," Nick assured him. "Keep going, guys. What happens next?" He was scribbling everything we said onto the giant notepad.

"He terrorizes the small town," I answered, "until the one person who can send him back, does. That tends to be how these movies go."

"The hero," Charlie said. "He can be, like, the long-lost descendant of the person who sealed the monster in long ago!"

"She," Betsy corrected him.

"What?" Charlie asked.

"She," Betsy, Ellie, and I repeated to him.

"We think the hero should be a girl," I explained to him.

"Right on," he agreed.

And so it continued until we had a really good, really creepy story! At one point I found myself looking around at all these kids and feeling really excited. They seemed excited, too, which made the air feel a little tingly. Like there was some magic in it. I mean, Betsy was agreeing with things I said! That had to be magic.

The rest of the day seemed to fly by as we planned what we were going to do each day until the premiere. It didn't seem like enough time to make a whole movie, but Nick told us that if we worked really hard, we could do it. I hoped he was right!

By the time I got home, I was absolutely bursting to tell Dad about our day. He and our dog Einstein were waiting for me on our back porch. This had become our nightly tradition in the summer, at least on the nights he didn't have to go work as a bouncer at the local nightclub. Two beers, one of the root variety, were each nestled in a red foam can cozy from our trip to the World's Largest Ball of Twine. In fancy scroll lettering, they read *Welcome to Twine Country*, which was surrounded by what looked like a grapevine, but instead of grapes, little balls of twine hung from the stems. Maybe it was all the fumes from riding on the back of Dad's motor-cycle for five hundred miles (or the delirium of having a numb butt for that long) but at the time we thought those drink holders were hilarious.

Einstein greeted me with his gruff little *Ruff!* and a

toothy dog smile. His nubby white tail wagged a zillion miles an hour when I picked him up and kissed his velvety little ears.

"Young Spielberg has arrived," Dad said, handing me my root beer. "How was it?"

"It was amazing!" I gushed. "I think we're going to have the best two weeks. Possibly ever."

I sat down with Einstein on my lap.

"Nick learn a lot at school?" Dad asked.

"Yes! And do you remember that girl from the old movie theater?"

"You'll have to be more specific than that."

"The one with the hair?" I said.

"Are all the other theater workers bald?"

"It doesn't matter. Her name is Ellie and she is also a counselor. She knows tons, too!"

"Cheers to that!"

The gentle *puft* of two pieces of foam tapping never sounded so good.

"Thanks again for letting me go," I added. "I'm sorry you're stuck with Ms. Watson. I hope she doesn't drive you totally bananas."

He took a sip before answering. "Nah, I actually think she'll work out. She's not that bad."

I shook my head to make sure I wasn't hallucinating. "We are talking about the same Ms. Watson, right? The one who tried for years and years and years to bust you for having powers? The one who was maybe gonna send me in to be dissected?"

"People mess up, Veri. You know that. I know that. And plus, if anyone should cut her some slack, it's us."

"Us? Cut *her* slack? Why?" I asked.

The sun was starting to set and its reflection made Dad's dark eyes sparkle. "Because she was right about us. We do have superpowers. And instead of just assuming that makes us dangerous, she learned the actual truth about what we're really like. And now she helps keep you safe."

He wasn't wrong.

"Well, when you put it that way . . . ," I said.

"When you see her around, just give her a chance, okay?" He nudged my knee with his.

I did my best noncommittal mumble.

"Pardon?"

He knew me too well. "Yes, Dad."

"Promise."

(Notice how that wasn't a question? More a command.)

"I promise."

"Or suffer a stinky death?"

"Or suffer a stinky death."

The pact was made, but I was sure I had the upper hand. With camp going on, it would be nearly impossible to have to spend any time with Ms. Watson whatsoever! I could keep this promise with no fear of stinky death.

CHAPTER THREE
MOVING PICTURES

I woke up super early and super excited about what was going to happen at camp that day. I was going to get to draw all day, working on storyboards! Nick and Ellie had explained that storyboarding is sort of like sketching out the movie before you film anything. Then everyone can see it and get a better feel for what we're all going for.

I had my pencils and big drawing pads all packed up and ready to go. Confession: The night before, I even spent some time coming up with ideas for how our monster could look. I knew we were supposed to brainstorm together, but I really wanted to impress Ellie and Nick. Is that so wrong?

My arms loaded to the max with supplies and my view completely blocked, I worked my way down the stairs. I could hear Dad whistling in the kitchen.

"Morning?" I said from behind a twenty-four-by-thirty-six-inch sketch pad. "Sounds like someone woke up on the right side of the bed. Or maybe in a parallel universe!"

It wasn't like Dad to whistle. Certainly not in the morning. That was a time for grumbling. Popular topics: the decibel level of our neighbor's sprinkler system; what he called "the Cereal Conspiracy," which is how cereal comes in this giant box but when you open it up the bag inside is only half-full; and the cost of whatever he was presently eating or drinking in "in my day" format. Example of all three rolled into one epic grumble: "In my day, your neighbor would never have sprinklers that were as loud as a dump truck, and you certainly wouldn't be paying four ninety-nine for half a box of Conspiracy Crunch Berries." Lucky for me, this morning he was too distracted by what I was carrying to badmouth any cereal moguls.

"Morning!" he said, then kissed me on the head and helped me gather up my heap of art supplies. "You running away to art school?"

"Not today," I said. "I get to storyboard at camp!"

"Oooh, nice!" Dad was enthused. "You'll kick butt at that." He started putting on his boots.

"I hope so," I said.

I grabbed two bananas from the fruit bowl on the kitchen table.

"So, what are *you* gonna kick butt at today?" I asked.

"Whaddaya mean?" He picked through the junk drawer looking for his keys.

"What's with the early-morning whistling?" I narrowed my eyes at him.

Keys found, he gave me a half smile. "What's with the two bananas?"

I opened my mouth to answer him, but then Charlie's head popped in through the front door.

"Ready to go?" Charlie asked. "Morning, Rik!"

"She's got her arsenal," Dad replied, handing Charlie an armful of my supplies. "And an extra banana."

On our way out the door, I smooched him on the cheek.

"Love you, kiddo," he called out after us.

"Love you!" I yelled back.

"I love you, Rik!" Charlie shouted back to him.

"Love you, little man. Enjoy your freakin' banana!"

"Your dad is a laugh." Charlie chomped on his banana as we walked to the theater.

"So what's up?" I asked. "You wanted to walk with me today even though you could've just gotten a ride with Nick."

"Well, yeah," Charlie said, and stuffed the second half of the banana in his mouth all at once. "Buh dere is sumding I nweed to twell woo."

"Can it wait until after you swallow?" I giggled.

Charlie gulped down the banana, then took a deep breath. "Listen. I, uh. . . ." He trailed off. Then he looked at the sky for a minute. Then his shoes. Then at his wrist, like he was wearing a watch, which he wasn't. What was with all the guys in my life acting so weird today?

"Charlie?" I asked.

"Oh!" He looked relieved as he spotted something in the distance. "Betsy!" He rushed to catch up with her, gesturing for me to follow.

What was with all the guys in my life acting SO VERY, VERY weird today?

I didn't catch up to Charlie and Betsy until we were just outside the theater. Nick, Ellie, Ted, and the campers were already there and splitting into smaller groups. Charlie sped ahead of us to join them.

Betsy had both her camera and a fancy video camera strapped around her neck. She looked as confused as I felt.

"What's with Charlie?" she asked me.

"I-I don't know," I whispered.

Dad was acting strange, Charlie was acting strange, and now Betsy's talking to me? I was beginning to worry that *I* was the one who woke up in a parallel universe.

"Guess we're in the same group today, eh, weirdo?" Betsy asked, gesturing to the other campers. Everyone else had teamed up except Charlie, who was standing with Nick, waiting for us.

"Hiya, guys," Nick greeted us. "Shall we get started?"

We sat down at a picnic table overlooking the river so Betsy and I could get a good look at our "set." Charlie wouldn't be able to practice his craft of acting until we had a script, so he was going to work with both Betsy and me to create a "vision" of what the movie should look like. Yep. You heard right! Charlie and me working *with* Betsy.

"Hey," I heard myself say after a too-long silence.

Betsy nodded back.

It felt like everything was moving in slow motion. The birds stopped singing. The wind stopped blowing. We couldn't even hear any of the other kids chatting in the distance. It was eerie silence.

Charlie coughed, then said, "So, maybe we should just get to work then?"

"Well, I was thinking that since we want to evoke a classic-film vibe, we should keep a lot of the angles low and dramatic. Shoot upward. That was pretty popular then. Gives everything more of a voyeuristic feel," Betsy said dryly and without taking a single breath.

Charlie and I looked at each other. I think we had just heard Betsy say more words in one sentence than we had heard from her our whole lives.

"That sounds perfect," I told her as I thought it through. It really did.

"Totally," Charlie agreed. "From an actor's perspective, I think having the camera out of my sight lines will greatly help the performance."

He said it so poshly that I had to stifle a giggle. I looked over and Betsy had raised one eyebrow. She thought it was funny, too.

Charlie caught both of our looks.

"Actors live their roles," he said defiantly. Then he broke out into a little laugh that the three of us shared. "Or so I've read."

"I was thinking the same thing," I told Betsy, feeling a little less nervous now that we had broken the ice, "and the more dramatic the angles are in the shots, the more—"

"—dramatic the scene will be," Betsy finished with a nod of agreement. She paused, then said, "Weird."

It seemed Betsy also found it odd that we were all agreeing.

"Well," she said as she stood back up, "before this gets any weirder, I'm gonna get started. I'll take some test shots for us to check out." She threw her camera bag over her shoulder and headed off.

"What is going on?" Charlie said, baffled.

"I don't know. It feels strange. Like something's wrong."

"Red flags."

"Yes! But does it feel wrong because she's tricking us? Or does it feel wrong because she's actually being kind of nice to us?"

"Only one way to find out," Charlie said, grinning.

"True," I agreed. "I guess I'll get started on some sketches so we can share them in a little bit. With Betsy. For fun."

Charlie laughed. "Sounds like a mildly terrifying plan! I'm gonna go see where I can be helpful."

Armed with the notes we'd taken at our story meeting the day before, I started drawing some monster concepts. After a few minutes, I went closer to the water to get a better view of some moss that I thought we could incorporate into our creature's costume. Nick came over and sat on a rock next to me and watched me work, which instantly made my palms sweaty.

"Great work, Veri," he said encouragingly. "Charlie said you were a really good artist, but I had no idea . . ."

He had never called me "Veri" before.

"Thanks," I said. I self-consciously rubbed my lip, then realized that I'd probably just smeared pencil on my face. Quickly, I used the hem of my T-shirt to wipe my mouth.

Looking up, I could see that Nick was trying to smother a laugh.

"Did I get it?" I sighed, giving in to my embarrassment.

"Yeah." He chuckled before milling through the binder he had with him. "Oh, here." He fished out a piece of paper with several large black squares across it. They looked like outlines, or empty frames.

"When you storyboard, it helps draw in small boxes that are the same dimensions as the screen. Pretend that this is what the camera sees."

"Oh, neat!" I took the paper. "Like each drawing is a shot the camera does?"

"Yep! And you don't have to be super detailed. Your job is just to get the message across so everyone can do their jobs better."

"Can do," I said.

He picked up another one of my sketchbooks and flipped through it, spotting the monster designs I had done the night before.

"You are really passionate about this, aren't you?" he asked.

I shrugged. "Yeah, I just had a lot of ideas that I wanted to get on paper."

"Well," Nick said, "Ellie and I were talking—would you be interested in being the director?"

I stopped sketching.

"Pardon? I think I just hallucinated."

Nick laughed. "This movie was your idea, Veri, and you

honestly have a vision for it, and you can instruct everyone through your storyboards. It's a great match and we know you could be a fantastic director."

"Whoa," I said quietly.

"Just say yes. I swear it'll work out perfectly."

"Yes?" I said. I was really unsure, but I could feel excitement and happiness starting to well up inside me. This was unreal! *Take it easy, Veri*, I told myself. The stupidpowers were starting to wake up. I could feel it.

"Great! Welcome aboard, Ms. Director."

He stood up and turned to go. "I'll leave you to it, then." He paused and turned back around. "Actually, I also wanted to say, you are handling this really well, Veri."

I nodded. "Thanks. It's all so . . . sudden." I wasn't used to so much praise, but it was growing on me.

"I know how hard Charlie is taking it, so I'm sure he appreciates you being cheerful."

Wait. What? I don't think we are talking about the same thing.

Nick continued, "He really doesn't want to move away, especially not so soon." He headed back to the group.

Every ounce of happiness that I had just felt dried up.

CHAPTER FOUR
EXPERIMENTAL FILM

Moving? Charlie was moving? I had stopped drawing a long time ago and one of my pencils had rolled into the water and was bobbing slowly out into the current. I knew I should grab it, but I couldn't move. I felt numb. Nick had solved the mystery of why Charlie had been acting so weird: He was leaving.

"Veri?" Charlie's voice cut through my brain fog. "We have a few things we'd love your opinion on—" He stopped short when he saw my face. "Oh, crackers."

Charlie sat on the same rock his brother had occupied a short while ago.

"Why didn't you tell me?" My voice shook.

"I tried. I tried all summer." Charlie kicked a rock into the water. "I just didn't want to . . . I-I dunno," he stammered. "Telling you made it seem real. Like it was really going to happen."

"But it *is* really going to happen?" I blinked back what was starting to feel like an impending flood of tears.

"Yeah," he quietly confirmed. "We leave a couple days after the premiere."

Using a turquoise hair tie I had around my wrist, I pulled my hair into the tightest ponytail ever.

My voice was getting wobblier by the word. "Why?"

Charlie looked pained, like we had put *his* hair in the tightest ponytail ever.

"My moms are outta research options here. That's what they told me, anyway."

Charlie's moms were both research scientists who worked on crazy secret projects all the time. Even their kids didn't know what they were up to in the heavily locked and sealed science lab at Charlie's house. It was all a secret. Maybe that was part of the problem.

He was uncharacteristically quiet. "They've been bickering a lot. Seems like they're really stressed-out because of it."

I crossed my arms and tried to put on a calm face. It wasn't working. I didn't know which one of us was going to cry first.

"Where?" I managed, but one of my tears broke through. I wiped my cheek on my shoulder.

"Upstate New York," he answered grimly. "They'll have access to New York City and be closer to Nick."

"That—that's like so, *so* far away, Charlie," I said, bracing for a sob.

"I know." His voice cracked.

Charlie went to put his hands on my shoulders, but upon realizing my right shoulder was wet from tears, he instead put one of his hands over my face and gently tapped it. The weird moment, in perfect Charlie fashion, broke the sad tension. We both laughed through wet eyes.

Unfortunately, it also unleashed the sadness I had been forcing back and sent my stupidpowers into a tizzy! Water poured from my eyes like I had a high-powered shower head behind each eye!

"Veri! I know you're sad, but everyone is going to see you!" Charlie tried desperately to block the view from the other campers. "Oh, crud. Nick is looking for us!"

"Charlie? Veri? What are you guys doing? Get up here!" Nick called as he walked toward us.

Charlie looked around for somewhere to hide me, but there was no shrub or tree in sight. The torrents from my eyes weren't slowing down. I couldn't stop!

"I'm really sorry about this," Charlie said, sighing. Then he pushed me into the river.

Five minutes later, I was sitting back at the picnic table drying off in the sun. The shock of the cold water had helped me break the hold of my powers. By the time I swam back to shore, they had fizzled out completely. Now I was just sad.

"Still not entirely sure how you managed to fall in, but whatever," Nick said as he offered me a towel and gave Charlie a side-eye. "Glad you're okay."

"There's a little good news," I said to Charlie once we were alone. "Nick and Ellie asked me to direct the movie!"

"Perfect, Veri! This is going to be absolutely smashing."

It *was* a little bit of good news for sure, but all I kept thinking about was Charlie leaving. It didn't seem like something that could be real. A day without Charlie? Many days without Charlie? It hurt my heart, not to mention my head, just trying to wrap my brain around the thought.

We worked through the rest of the afternoon, but I was a bit of a zombie. Being in a daze was probably to my advantage, since I ended up having to talk to Betsy a lot. Under normal circumstances, I don't think I could have handled that. Right now, being afraid of something as basic as a sparring match with Betsy felt cozily familiar.

"If Max doesn't want the costume in the water, we could always go out into the river and film the act of coming out of the water, so it looks like we're showing the monster's point of view," Betsy told me.

I nodded. "That's a good idea."

"Here." She swung her hand toward me and I flinched. "It's just a Kleenex."

"Uh, thanks," I said, taking it. I had been leaking tears on and off since Charlie's confession.

"No problem," she said, still not looking at me. I was beginning to wonder if she had also been weirded out by how much we agreed earlier. I couldn't blame her. This was very new territory for both of us.

I sketched some more ideas for our monster, since the next day I'd be working with Max on costumes, building what I drew. Normally that would be cause for a huge celebration, but I just kept thinking about Charlie. We had spent almost every day of our lives together. How in the heck would I survive without him? Who would push me in the river when I needed to be pushed in the river?

When camp was over for the day, Nick asked if I wanted a ride home with him and his brother. I did. I wanted to spend as much time with Charlie as I could. In fact, I wanted to hijack the car and drive Charlie and me somewhere far away. It was a really short ride, but we said nothing. Nick kept looking at us in the rearview mirror.

"Guys?" he inquired as he pulled up in front of my house.

Charlie kicked the back of Nick's seat. "She didn't know, jerkburger."

Nick turned around to face us. "Oh man. I'm so sorry. I didn't mean to . . . We had talked about it last night, Charlie—that you had to tell her this morning."

Charlie seethed. "Well, I didn't."

I opened the door to get out. "It's okay, guys. Nick didn't mean anything by it, Charlie." I forced a small smile. "Text me later?" I asked.

"Whether you like it or not," he said, and grinned.

Suddenly I felt like I was going to cry again. I shut the door and waved as I ran inside the house.

"Veri?" Dad called from the back porch.

"Coming," I yelled as I slipped off my still-wet sneakers. I ran into the bathroom and changed out of my damp clothes into pajamas. After the day I had, I deserved early pajamas and a very big hug from my dad.

But the few minutes alone set my brain back into spiral mode. I needed to talk to someone before my powers went crazy again.

"Oh, Daddy," I cried as I stepped onto the deck.

"Kiddo?" Dad stood up, instantly worried.

I started running up to him, but I stopped before I got into hug range.

"Well, this is already awkward," an uptight voice announced.

There she was: Ms. Watson. Sitting on my deck. Petting my dog. Drinking my root beer.

"They're moving that soon, huh?" Dad asked, smoothing back one of my wild curls. I had explained to him and Ms. Watson (but mainly him) about Charlie moving, but it didn't make me feel that much better. At least I was at home, with people who knew about my powers, so I didn't have to *also* worry about the little storm clouds circling around us, threatening to rain at any second.

Dad had explained to me that they had also had a rough day at work, so he invited Ms. Watson over for a drink to decompress. I know it's awful, but I didn't really hear what he said about why they had a bad day. He said something about "electronic filing" and my brain checked out. I had other things to think about. Mainly the imminent departure of my best friend.

"He can't go," I moaned. "Who am I supposed to be friends with now? Betsy?!"

"I'm so sorry, Ver." Dad consoled me. "Unfortunately, parents have to make hard decisions like this. Sounds like there isn't any work for them here. They can't take care of Charlie if they don't have any money."

"They could get different jobs. Here," I explained. "Why do they have to be fancy research scientists?"

"Science is important work, McGowan," Ms. Watson chimed in. "And look around. Is it really a surprise that there's nothing here for them to research?"

My annoyance at Ms. Watson became quite visible. My sad clouds churned so much they developed little lightning storms. They got so ferocious that one cloud bounced against Ms. Watson's head. Then she got in the line of fire from one of the minibolts!

"Ow! Little help here?" Ms. Watson asked Dad, eyeing the cloud that kept bumping her.

"Probably a good time to just be quiet," Dad offered. I love my dad.

He gave me a big squeeze. "I'm sorry there isn't anything I can do to fix this."

I spent the rest of the night in a haze. I moped in the living room, stupidpowers storm clouds in tow. Ms. Watson left. Dad and I ate something for dinner. I told him about my big promotion to director. There was TV watching. It wasn't

until I was in bed that I started to process thoughts again. If Charlie's parents had something interesting and scientific to research, they could stay, right? Problem: It wasn't like Pearce was this hotbed of interesting stuff. Nothing of note had come from this town in, well, ever. Of course, I mean, other than my powers.

But that was the thing. I was researchable. And, from a scientific point of view, my powers were very interesting. If I told Charlie's parents about my powers, they might just stay! They might also want to remove all of my bones or something, but maybe letting them experiment on me was the only shot I had of keeping Charlie here.

What if I told his moms what I could do?

CHAPTER FIVE

DEAL BREAKER

"Absolutely not," Charlie said, incredulous. His voice rang against the old tiled walls of the theater's kitchen, where we were working on costumes.

I'd expected a better, happier response to my plan from Charlie. If I let his moms experiment on me, he could stay!

"It's not like they'd make me a lab rat, Charlie," I explained. "They like me!"

While Max, the costumer, had stepped away to dig around the old costume closet, I decided to work on convincing Charlie that it was a good idea to tell his moms about my powers. It wasn't going so well. Charlie pulled the trigger on the hot-glue gun, sending a long stream of glue onto the old Batman cowl Max had brought in for us to use as a base for our river monster costume. Charlie then smooshed a piece of moss on top of the glue.

"No," he said definitively. "We don't know what they would do! It's not like they've ever been offered something like this before. I mean, usually they get all giddy and self-important if they find a single, tiny, stupid mutated cell. They talk to any scientific journal who will listen!" He furrowed his brow and glued a piece of plastic seaweed to one of Batman's ears. "And you are one giant, in-the-flesh mutated cell!"

I swatted his shoulder. "Excuse me?"

He finally looked up at me, the Charlie gleam returning to his eye. "I mean that in the best way possible." He took a deep breath. "Listen, all I'm saying is that things could get out of control pretty easily. After their big artificial slug-excretion discovery last year they don't need money, but they *do* want another big discovery that they can tell people about."

I grimaced. "I still can't believe people put slug goo in their cosmetics."

"Well, now they can put *slug-free* slug goo in their cosmetics."

I thought about the (non-sluggy) stuff Charlie had said. "I guess I do need to be careful. It isn't just me. Dad could get found out, too. Part of this deal has to be that I stay anonymous. I mean, scientists keep test subjects' identities secret all the time, right?" I asked.

Charlie shrugged. "I dunno, and it's not worth the risk, Veri. What if they run tests on you that somehow make your powers worse?"

I hadn't thought of that.

"There has to be a way, Charlie," I practically begged. "We can't let you just move."

"This isn't the way." His gleam was gone. "And your dad would kill all of us."

"How's it going?" Ellie interrupted. Her periwinkle hair now had dark purple roots.

"Not too shabby," Charlie said. He handed her the mask and my sketch of the river monster.

"That looks great!" she exclaimed, admiring Charlie's hot-glue handiwork. "River Monster Batman was my favorite action figure growing up."

Charlie and I laughed.

"Actually, Charlie, Nick said you are interested in sound design?" Ellie asked.

"Sound effects? Yes!" Charlie perked up immensely.

"Cool." Ellie beamed. "We borrowed some sound equipment from the community college, like boom mics and stuff, if you want to come play." She paused. "I mean, *learn*."

Charlie was already out of his seat.

"We'll find someone else to give you a hand here, Veronica," Ellie reassured me. "I'm pretty sure Max is done rifling around in the costume closet."

"Okay," I said. "Have fun, Charlie!"

A few minutes later, I was joined by Ted and Max.

"What y'all may not know about your pal Ted is that I have some excellent costuming skills," Ted said, smiling broadly.

"You've worked on films before?" Max asked hopefully. He had brought back a stack of hats, which he was balancing on his head. I was pretty sure they were for him, not the movie.

"No, man, but I have made all my own costumes for the past five years of Burning Man!" he said proudly.

"Aren't most people naked at that festival?" I asked.

"Not all the time," he answered. "Sometimes we wear feathers."

I tried to share a look with Max, but he clearly hadn't found the same amusement in what Ted had said. I wished Charlie hadn't gone off to break celery and hope it sounded like bones cracking or whatever special sound effects techniques he was learning.

I spotted Charlie on the other side of the park. He was smiling and having a great time waving a bamboo reed through the air, while I sat there with no one to share a look with. Was this how the rest of my life was going to be? Alone? With no one who understood me? While Charlie made all sorts of friends and forgot about that troublesome one back in that dumb small town?

I couldn't let that happen. I had to do something.

At the end of camp that day Ellie had invited everyone to the movie theater for a free screening of one of the silly horror classics, *Beast from Haunted Cave*. I would have loved to go, but instead . . . I lied. I said I had to go straight home, and then I went to the Weathers residence. Knowing Charlie and Nick wouldn't be home for seventy-five minutes was the best insurance I could ask for.

I stood outside the sleek, modern house. Charlie's moms, Lucia and Daphne, were some of the most stylish people I knew. I guess that's what happens when you are always traveling the world for conferences and speaking tours.

Still, I was really nervous and not at all sure this was a sane idea. Maybe they would take me with them after they dissected me. Or at least parts of me. Ha. I made a joke to myself that didn't help me feel better at all. It didn't matter, though, because I knew I had to do this, and I had to hurry. I only had so much time before Charlie got back. I didn't want him to get in the way. Especially since he was going to be so mad at me! But I was acting for the greater good. He couldn't be mad at me after his moms decided to stay.

I rang the doorbell, which was quickly answered by their housekeeper, John.

"Charlie isn't here," he told me, already closing the door.

"I'm not here for Charlie." I grabbed the doorknob. "I need to talk to his parents. It's important."

John raised an eyebrow but said nothing as he let me in. He then pointed toward the living room, silently directing me to sit.

While I waited, I looked at the pictures on the fireplace mantel. There was a great one of little Nick holding a baby Charlie.

Charlie and I didn't spend a lot of time at his house. I guess it was because it felt a little sterile there. Can a house be too clean? Too quiet? My house was always noisy, whether it was my dad blasting music or the rage-inducing *tick-tick-zwiiisssh* of the neighbor's sprinklers. Charlie's place was silent most of the time. Like, pin-drop silent. His moms were nice and all—especially Lucia, who was warm and open—but Dr. Weathers could be a bit . . . *terse*, I think is the right word. I guess it's all in the name, right? My dad has all my friends call him by his first name, Rik, so I had assumed I should call Charlie's parents by their first names. Wrong! That did not go over so well. Lucia didn't mind at all, but Daphne instantly corrected me, "Doctor Weathers." It was scary. I mean, I'm grateful that at least Lucia didn't mind me being so informal, because if they both had to be called Dr. Weathers, things would get really confusing. See, this is why everyone should go by their first names.

Come to think of it, why does Ms. Watson still call me "McGowan"? What does she call my dad?

My deep thoughts were broken by the *beep-beep-beep* sound of the lab door unlocking.

"Veronica!" Lucia called out, her tanned arms open wide to hug me.

"Is Charlie okay?" Dr. Weathers asked.

"Yes. He's fine. Nick, too," I said, my voice slightly muffled through Lucia's shoulder.

Lucia sat with me on the white leather couch, while Dr. Weathers sat across from us in a clear plastic chair.

Dr. Weathers picked up a large hardcover book called *Meta Existentialism* from the end table and opened it. She gave it a quick glance, like she was planning on reading while we talked, then tucked a piece of her short, pale blond hair behind her ear. "Great. What can we do for you?"

I felt Lucia's hand rest on the back of my neck. She could tell I was scared.

"Are *you* okay?" she asked, her hazel eyes soft. "I'm sure the news of us moving has been very hard on you."

"Well," my voice creaked, "that's actually what I'm here about. I want to make you a deal so you'll stay."

"Oh, sweetie," Lucia cooed.

Dr. Weathers stood up suddenly and slammed the book shut. "This is a waste of time. It is what it is, Veronica."

My nerves were so fried that the loud *thwat!* from the book sent me over the edge! Stupidpowers activated and every picture on the mantel came to life. Every photo let out little startled screams over and over again, but in my voice! Needless to say, Lucia and the doctor were freaked out.

"What was that?!" Lucia picked up the same picture of Nick and Charlie I had held earlier and turned it over to inspect it.

"Some kind of prank," Dr. Weathers scolded me. "Where are the speakers?"

"It-it wasn't a prank," I stammered. "It was me."

Lucia stopped investigating the pictures and looked at me. She was listening. Dr. Weathers was not. She was now on her hands and knees trying to figure out how I had rigged the pictures to make noise. "Must be Bluetooth or something . . . ," she mumbled.

I decided to go on. "So, last year all this weird stuff started happening to me. Like, um, remember when there was that fire at school? Uh, that was because I got upset and breathed fire. I, uh, also have turned to stone, and um, I shrink sometimes or grow a shell. It's really embarrassing,

but also sometimes these little hearts can follow me around. Oh! And just yesterday I cried, like, rivers of water. And, uh, one time I wiped the whole school's memory. Accidentally! Totally accidentally."

Thinking about all my powers over the last few months made me relive a lot of them. It felt like all of those emotions were spinning around in me, like I was a clothes dryer. At this point I realized that Dr. Weathers and Lucia were now both listening intently, mouths agape.

"Sorry. That's a lot to take in," I said.

Lucia pointed behind me. I turned around to discover a wild mishmash of my stupidpowers were now in their living room! Random hearts bounced around with rain clouds over their heads, tiny fire-breathing turtles walked around my feet, and both my hands had shrunk to one-sixteenth their size!

"Oh boy." I laughed nervously. "Well, there you go. I think I might be the perfect research subject."

Seeing how entranced they were, I reached out my tiny hand, offering a shake. "So you wanna make a deal?"

CHAPTER SIX
SINKING FEELING

Surprisingly, Charlie's parents had agreed with me that I should be the one to tell him that I went through with my plan, and that's what I was about to do. I had waited all morning through our production meeting where I showed off the River Monster costume and got feedback on the set designs that I was going to work on with Charlie and the tech kids today. Nick sent us off to "take ten," which is fancy movie talk for a ten-minute break. Everyone else went outside or to the bathroom, so Charlie and I had the whole auditorium to ourselves.

"What did you do?" Charlie asked.

"What?"

"You have your guilty face on," he pointed out.

"I didn't know I had a 'guilty face,'" I replied.

"So, spit it out," he said as he pulled himself up on the stage. I followed.

The stage was littered with props and set pieces the *Peter Pan* cast had neglected to put away the night before. I gently kicked Captain Hook's hat, sending it coasting across the set.

"You aren't going to be happy at first, but *then* you'll be *really* happy," I said. "In the future."

He leaned against a huge set piece that was made to look like the roots of a tree; it had a hidden compartment for the Lost Boys to pop out of during one of the scenes in the play.

"Tell me you didn't," he warned.

"I did," I confessed.

"Veronica!" Charlie snapped.

"But we made a deal, Charlie—they aren't going to tell anyone about me! Their findings will be completely anonymous!"

"I can't believe you! We talked about this!"

"You! You talked about it! You told me what I could and couldn't do!" Now I was getting mad.

"Unbelievable," he muttered.

Ooh. This boy was looking to get it.

"You're welcome, by the way," I said. "You get to stay here now."

"Really bad things could happen to you, Veri," he replied.

I spoke before I thought. "Well, nothing could be as bad as you leaving."

The truth of those words began to sink in.

Charlie sighed and hopped off the stage. "Just give me a few minutes to process this," he said.

"Fine."

Once he was gone, I climbed inside the Lost Boys' tree roots and lay down on my back. It reeked of spray paint and Styrofoam. I closed my eyes and tried to ignore the sinking feeling in my stomach. Was Charlie right? Was this a bad idea? Did I just make the biggest mistake of my life? The sinking dread in my stomach was getting stronger and stronger. Heavier and heavier. If I messed up, it would really hurt Dad. I didn't even think about how I'd keep him safe. Oh, Veronica Daisy McGowan, what did you do? Could I feel any lower?

My eyes popped open. Wait, I really was sinking! My powers had caused the floor around the tree to turn into quicksand, and I was going down with it—fast!

Sand was pouring in through every hole in the fake tree and filling it up faster than I could move! I knew I needed to pull myself out before the whole tree got swallowed up by the sand with me inside it!

I tried pushing down as hard as I could with my feet, but my leg just became more deeply trapped in the sand. The more I struggled, the farther and farther I sank until the sand started creeping over my shoulders. As it neared my chin, I tried to let out a scream, but the sand was moving too fast and almost filled my mouth. I was losing sight of the opening at the top of the fake tree. This was getting really serious. *What did they do in movies when they got trapped in quicksand?* I tried to remember. *They had to chill out and not flail! I have to try to float on my back!*

I took a deep breath before the sand covered my head. Slowly I moved my legs forward. It was so hard to go slow, especially with the sand rising every second, but soon I could feel myself rising back up! Within a few seconds I was on my back at the top of the quicksand. Relieved, I pushed myself

using the side wall of the tree and was finally able to get my footing and pull myself out of the highest opening in the tree.

That seemed to make the sand move even faster to engulf the fake tree. My foot cleared the opening just before the tree was sucked under completely. I slid backward on my butt and watched as the floor sealed itself up right before my eyes. It was like it had never happened. Except a giant piece of the Peter Pan set was gone.

Crash!

I heard Charlie's voice echo up the stairwell. "What just happened?!"

I ran down the stairs into the kitchen, where Charlie had apparently been stress-eating a box of cereal until a large fake tree had oozed through the ceiling and crashed haphazardly on top of the stove and refrigerator.

Spoon still in hand, Charlie asked, "That was you?"

"Yeah," I admitted. "Uh, we should probably get out of here."

We met everyone back upstairs for our task of the day—casting! Which meant auditions. I was so happy that I wasn't going to be on the stage today trying out. Doing all this production design work felt a lot better than trying to impress people. It was, like, one of the best realizations I had ever had.

"It's important that we are professional about this," Nick said. "That means we don't whisper among ourselves or make mean comments about people who audition."

"Don't be a jerk, essentially," Ellie summed up.

"They should be here any second," Nick said, checking his phone.

We already knew that a few of the campers were going to audition, but Rashida had also put flyers up around town for non-campers to come try out, too. Nick and Ellie thought everyone should watch auditions so we could learn how to cast the right people in the right roles. We waited another fifteen minutes, but no one showed up. Until . . .

"Um, hi?" a familiar voice came from the doorway.

It was Hun Su, the prettiest girl at Pearce Middle School.

"Well, come on in," Nick invited her.

"Great! I'm Hun Su." She gave her perfect, dazzlingly white smile and looked around the room. "Am I late?"

"Uh, no," Ellie answered. "It appears you are the only non-camper to audition."

Charlie leaned over and whispered to me, "I hope we get a better crowd for the actual movie."

Hmm. Charlie was right. We were really going to have to work hard if we wanted to make great cinema and wow our prospective audience next week.

Hun Su sat next to me while Nick dug through his bag, looking for a script for Hun Su to read from. "We don't really have an official, completed script yet; we're more working it out as we go, but I did pull together a scene to read . . ."

"Hi, Hun Su," I said.

"Hey . . . Victoria," she said cheerfully.

"Veronica," I corrected her. For the eight hundred millionth time.

She cringed. "Sorry!"

Hun Su auditioned, of course, for our lead. The scrappy, self-reliant heroine, Jessie, who saves everyone and sends the monster back to its evil realm. Charlie, along with Avery, auditioned for whatever roles they could get cast in. When the auditions were over, everyone who had tried out left the room so the rest of us could deliberate. Since it was such a small cast anyway, I thought we'd be able to slip each person into a role, no problem. Of course, Charlie would be the monster.

"I think Avery should be the monster," Betsy declared as soon as the auditioners were gone.

"What?" I blurted out. "Avery? Before today, have you heard him say a single word? Charlie is the perfect monster."

"*Pffft.*" Betsy rolled her eyes. "Of course you think that, since he's your boyfriend."

"He's not my boyfriend!" I objected. Then I looked at Nick, who had both eyebrows raised. "Listen," I said calmly, trying to collect myself, "Charlie is the right height for the costume. He's also really loud and good at gross sounds." I paused, trying not to say it again, but I did anyway. "And he's not my boyfriend." I looked at Ellie for help.

"We are going to do a vote. Unless anyone else wants to suggest someone else to play the monster?" Ellie asked.

Okay. I could handle this. With Ellie, Nick, and Ted, it would be four against three!

"Who votes for Charlie?" Ellie asked.

I raised my hand and then looked to Ellie, Ted, and Nick, who weren't moving.

"You aren't going to vote for your brother?" I asked Nick.

"I'm not voting for anyone. None of us are. It's your movie," Nick explained, gesturing to all of us.

And just like that, my vision of what the movie could be had its first casualty.

Nick had errands to run after camp, so Charlie and I walked home, which was actually better. It gave us some time to talk about his moms' impending research on me.

"I should have known," Charlie said. "Mom was giddy last night! I don't think I've seen her crack a smile since Bill Nye came back to TV." After a pause, he asked, "So, what's the plan, then?"

"I'm not really sure," I said. "I guess they are going to look into some stuff, and then I'll come over on Saturday and Sunday for some 'preliminary tests.' That's what they called them."

Charlie exhaled all the air out of his body. "That doesn't sound terrifying at all."

"Charlie! It's your moms!" I rolled my eyes at him.

"Dude, when they are in Science Mode, they are no one's moms," he said in all seriousness.

"It'll be fine," I said, more to reassure myself than him.

"And we are not telling Rik?" Charlie asked.

I thought about it for a minute. It had been so great to not have Big Secrets from Dad for the past few weeks. I wasn't too jazzed to start lying to him again. But there was absolutely no way he'd ever agree to any of this. I sighed. "No. No, no, no, no. Noooo. Unfortunately. No."

"Agreed." Charlie added, "I'd like to live to see my teens."

"He's at the club tonight. Wanna watch a movie?" I asked.

Charlie nodded. "Sure. And thanks to you, it won't be one of our last ones together."

"We won't *draw the curtain* on our friendship?" I smiled, wiggling my eyebrows.

He laughed. "Puns like that might make me rethink not moving."

When I arrived at camp early that next morning, there was already a bluster of angry activity. Charlie, Nick, and I walked into the theater at the same time.

Much to our surprise, in full *Peter Pan* regalia, the summer stock players were onstage. Most looked exhausted. Peter Pan himself was holding a Starbucks cup.

"What the—" Nick said.

"This is a closed re-hear-sal!" a man across the room said in singsong from behind a script.

"Mr. Stephens," Charlie and I grumbled in unison.

Nick heard us. "Who?"

"Our really annoying drama teacher. Started last year. He's also really pretentious," Charlie said.

"Like *really* pretentious," I agreed.

"Did we mention he's really pretentious?" Charlie joked.

I joined in, "Yeah, Nick, Mr. Stephens—don't know if you knew, but he's really pretentious."

Nick and Ellie laughed.

"Guess I should take care of this," Nick said before heading over to Mr. Stephens.

"*Eew*," a low voice next to me muttered.

It was Betsy, who was voicing her own disgust of the Pretentious One. I was still completely unsure what to do about having one of my greatest enemies around all the time. She was right next to me. What's the protocol for when you run into a bear in the woods?

Before I could back away slowly, Betsy moved on, sitting down next to Ted, who offered her a high five. She left him hanging until he abandoned all hope.

The rehearsal stopped completely as the gestures and sounds from Nick and Mr. Stephens's conversation got louder and more dramatic. Ellie, who was on the other side of me, took a step toward them, like she was ready to dive into the fight at any moment.

"What are you even talking about?" Nick asked. "Why—more importantly *how*—would any of these kids move your tree all the way downstairs and put it on top of the fridge?"

Mr. Stephens looked deeply surprised. "You're saying an adult did this? An adult attempted to destroy a valuable and essential piece of art?"

"Valuable? Art? I'm not saying that." Nick wearily rubbed his forehead.

"Well, the only 'adults' here are you and the girl and the

thing over there." Mr. Stephens pointed to Ellie and then Ted, who had fallen asleep despite the bustle.

Meanwhile, Charlie and I looked at each other, wide-eyed and guilt ridden.

"I should say something. Confess or whatever," I whispered to Charlie.

"No," he whispered back, "Nick has it under control."

Mr. Stephens's voice boomed through the room. "This is *my* theater. What I say goes!"

"It's the community's theater, Richard," Nick said, and sighed.

"Well, the community wants to see professional-grade theater at a discount price and that is what I give them. Not whatever swill your scraggly little ragtag film crew can cook up." Mr. Stephens said *film* like it left a bad taste in his mouth.

Ellie took three steps toward them.

"Besides," Mr. Stephens continued slightly quieter, "I've seen what most of those kids can do, and it ain't much. They are not professional grade."

Nick opened his mouth to reply, but Ellie beat him to it.

"Well, Mr. Pretentious—" she started.

I muffled my laugh with my hand, but Charlie let out a big snort with reckless abandon.

Ellie continued, "Until we are told *by the community* to leave this theater, we won't. You'll have to share."

Mr. Stephens sneered at her. "Well, you won't get the stage. The auditorium is *ours* and off-limits to *all* of you for destroying our masterpiece of a set!"

"We are going to one of the rehearsal rooms, and we are going to be *very* loud," Ellie said with a smile. She turned and gestured for us to follow her.

"Well, there ya go," Nick said to Mr. Stephens. He shot Ellie a look of pride.

Down in the rehearsal room, things weren't quite as posh or well maintained. There were exposed water pipes, peeling paint, and a very annoyed Ellie.

"Ugh. Let that jerk be a warning to all of you—don't peak in high school!" she exclaimed.

"Hear! Hear!" Charlie agreed.

"Take a chill, little camper. No need to go kayaking on those white-water waves," Ted said in his soothing voice.

Betsy let out a loud, annoyed sigh.

He shut up.

"So, what do we do?" I asked.

The room went silent for a minute until Ellie lit up and said, "We make our movie. For the community."

Nick nodded in agreement. He obviously knew what Ellie meant.

"Brilliant," he encouraged.

"What?" Betsy asked.

Ellie explained, "They open next Friday, and now so do we. We're going to have a *community* screening for our movie."

There was a collective gasp from all of us campers.

"And we'll see who gets more people in seats."

Ellie hadn't been kidding around. Our instructions were crisp and concise.

"We need you to design posters for our movie," Ellie directed me. "Rashida will put them up as soon as you're done."

"One thing," Betsy observed. "Having our viewing

party at Nick's was fine when there was just us. Where are we gonna fit all of Pearce for a premiere? They've got the stage that night."

Ellie beamed. "I happen to be pretty tight with the owner of an actual movie theater."

Holy cow! Our movie being shown in an *actual* movie theater? Maybe me accidentally sinking the tree into the basement was a good thing after all!

I quickly sketched a poster for our new premiere. After we had made fifty copies of them, I took the original to Ellie, who was more than happy to hand deliver the announcement to Mr. Stephens. Charlie and I went with her for our own sheer enjoyment.

Mr. Stephens looked over the poster with a smirk.

"This is very . . . cute. You're on."

Then he crushed the poster and threw it over his shoulder.

I picked up my crumpled artwork.

"Aww man," I sighed.

"Sorry," Ellie apologized. "We shouldn't have given him the original."

Charlie took it from me and did his best to flatten it out.

"No, it's good. Just another reason to show him what's what," I insisted.

"So, you'll be over in the morning?" Charlie asked as we helped Avery into the monster suit. He was trying it on for the first time. It was the end of the day and threatening rain, so it was humid as heck and Avery was sweating like crazy.

"Yeah," I answered, pulling at the moss-covered scuba suit, "they said eight a.m. Before I eat, so they can take blood."

Avery whipped his head around to look at me, puzzled. He said nothing, of course.

"Ha!" I fake laughed. "Just seeing if you were paying attention, Avery."

Charlie handed me the monster mask and I slid it over Avery's head. I shrugged my shoulders and mouthed "Oops!" to Charlie.

"Well that was fun!" Charlie joked as Avery waddled off to have Betsy look at him through the camera.

I giggled. "He's so quiet! I totally forgot he was there!"

"You nervous?" Charlie asked.

"About tomorrow or about directing this movie?" I asked. "The short answer is that everything is freaking me out."

It was true. I was really nervous about everything. Here I was, about to say *Action!* for the first time, with everyone watching me and expecting me to know all the answers. To bring this whole movie together so we could prove our awesomeness in the battle with Mr. Stephens. I was also about to subject myself to experiments. I had no idea what they would be, or what they would do to me, let alone if I would make it out of them okay. Considering all the damage my powers could cause, I wanted to believe that nothing could make them worse, but who could guarantee that? What if I got stuck constantly having powers? I'd never be able to leave the house again! That is, if the house didn't explode.

"Veri? Ready?" Charlie asked.

I had totally zoned out.

"Sure." I wiped my dirty palms on my overalls. "Let's make a movie."

CHAPTER SEVEN
THE LAST SUPPER

Dad was under the impression that Charlie and I would be working at his house all day on movie stuff. Where did he get that impression? Me. Lying. Again. It still felt really wrong. It was never a good scene when I lied to Dad, and, honestly, it rarely worked out, but that was a risk I was willing to take. Having Dad be mad at me was a small price to pay to have Charlie stay. But maybe Dad would never find out anyway. Things could go absolutely perfectly and be amazing! Perfect and amazing. Perfect and amazing.

I repeated these words over and over in my head as I sat on a hospital-style bed Dr. Weathers had rolled into the lab.

"We just want you to be comfortable," Lucia noted after she saw me look at it, worried.

"I guess I won't worry until you bring in a straitjacket," I said, and laughed nervously.

Lucia smiled, but Dr. Weathers didn't react. Instead, she asked, "Have you ever been struck by lightning?"

"Me? No," I said. "But Ms. Watson was accidentally hit with my mini lightning bolts."

Charlie, who was sitting in the corner of the room, giggled.

"Charlie. We had an agreement," Dr. Weathers said without looking at him.

He covered his mouth with his hand, doing his best to stay silent.

"Okay, Veronica, I'm going to draw your blood right now to do some basic testing on it," Lucia said, putting on purple latex gloves. "You okay?"

She wrapped a plastic strap around my bicep, causing the veins in the bend of my inner elbow to bulge. I nodded, but I wasn't feeling okay. I had failed to mention to them that I was deathly afraid of needles. Had been since I was a baby. I didn't want to mess this deal up, but all my tough self-talk wasn't chilling me out one bit.

"You'll just feel a little pinch . . ." Lucia trailed off as she brought the needle toward my right arm.

I held my breath and looked away as the needle was about to pierce my skin, but instead of feeling a pinch, I heard a gentle *tink!* sound.

"Well, that's interesting." Lucia marveled.

I looked back and saw that the needle was bent! My arm was now coated in what looked like gold! My stupid-powers had fired again, trying to save me from . . . I dunno. Charlie's moms?

"Very interesting, indeed," Dr. Weathers agreed, making a note on her tablet. "Veronica, can you make it go away?"

"I wish," I nervously replied. "It'll eventually wear off, and sometimes it helps if I calm down, but I, uh, don't see that happening soon. I'm really nervous."

"Oh, no reason to be nervous, sweetheart," Lucia reassured me.

"She has every reason to be concerned," Dr. Weathers said flatly. "These abilities are unheard of."

Lucia rubbed my back while shooting daggers at her wife. "She is in the best hands."

"Just stating facts," Dr. Weathers said.

The metal was spreading through my shoulder and chest.

Charlie rushed up to me, eager to get a closer look. "Dude, you're turning into a droid!" he said, tapping on my arm.

"Don't. That feels really weird," I told him.

Oblivious, Charlie said, "Like, you're becoming the Terminator!"

Lucia and I shared a look.

"What?" Charlie asked. "I mean, she's okay. You're okay, Veri, aren't you?"

I was okay. Things like this happened to me all the time. Just never in front of doctors who were trying to suck out my blood and figure out how I worked.

I nodded.

"You just need to relax, sweetie," Lucia reminded me. "It's just us. We are all friends."

"I wasn't trying to be . . . this," I pointed to my metal appendage.

"I know. I know. A few deep breaths maybe?"

"Yeah," I agreed.

"In through the nose, out through the mouth," Charlie

directed me in his most Zen-like voice. It made me giggle, which helped tremendously. "Do it!"

I did. A few deep breaths and I was still scared, but less so. Looking at Charlie, you'd think he just spent a week at a spa. His eyes were heavy and he was fighting back a yawn.

"So comfy," he mumbled. He took his seat and leaned back, and his eyelids dropped like curtains.

"That kid can sleep anywhere," Lucia said with a laugh. She grabbed a spare lab coat and covered Charlie with it. "So, how are you feeling?" She had turned her attention back to me.

I wiggled my fingers at her. They were turning back to flesh. "Better."

"Great! Maybe we can try to get that blood sample again?"

"Sure," I said, my voice cracking as Dr. Weathers reappeared with a new syringe.

"There's nothing to be scared of," Dr. Weathers insisted.

"I'm not scared," I lied.

I'm not scared, I'm not scared, I'm not scared, I repeated to myself as I shut my eyes tightly, waiting for the death pinch of the needle. Waiting. Waiting. I peeked out of one eye to see what was taking so long. That was a bad idea. I caught a peeper full of the syringe as it was going into my arm. It felt like the room was spinning around me. I was so woozy. It was getting dark . . .

"Ah!" I shot awake, sitting straight up in an absolute panic.

"It's okay! You're okay!" Lucia said, gently grabbing my shoulders. "You just fainted. You were only out for a few seconds."

"Ack!" Charlie woke up at the commotion. "It's not even my gerbil!" he mumbled, still half-asleep.

I was taking some slow, deep breaths. At least I had survived the blood draw!

"Oh, hey!" Charlie greeted us, now fully awake. "You okay, Ver—whoa!"

I looked up to see what he had *whoa*ed at. "Whoa," I echoed.

The lab was a mess. There was water dripping from a half-deflated rain cloud in the corner. One wall was peppered with scorch marks and there was a giant blob of green goo encasing the exam lamp.

"I did that?" I asked.

Lucia nodded. "Right after you fainted."

"How did you make me do all these things?"

"Yeah, we haven't even seen the green Jell-O power before," Charlie remarked.

"We didn't do anything. It just all came out at once," Lucia explained.

"It would be highly unethical for us to examine you while you were unconscious. Unless we had preapproval, of course," Dr. Weathers chimed in. She was putting a sample of the green blob into a petri dish.

"Have you ever had your symptoms display while you've been sleeping?" Lucia asked.

"*Um*," I thought. "Yeah, my very first power. Hearts. Did you see them here?"

"Hearts? No."

"Well, they were in my room when I woke up when this all first started." That was all I wanted to say about that. I definitely didn't want to tell them it was directly after I had a dream about my crush.

"Well, if it hasn't happened since, maybe we can speculate that she is returning to her precondition state?" Dr. Weathers said to Lucia.

Charlie and I looked hopefully at each other.

"But you would think that would be indicated by a lessening of symptoms, not a surge," Lucia replied.

"True."

Dr. Weathers typed more notes in her tablet. "It could also be that in a modified sleep state, her condition may trigger the release of anything that was pent up."

"Pent up?" I asked, but neither scientist was listening to me. They were both deep in thought.

"Hello?" I smile and waved, trying to get their attention.

"Oh, sorry, Veri," Lucia apologized. "Science brain took over."

"Oh, crud," I said, spotting the clock. It was almost dinnertime and I knew Dad would have questions if I wasn't there on time. "I need to go. Can I go?" I asked Lucia.

"Of course, as long as you're feeling up to it?" Lucia asked as she looked me over.

"I feel fine now. Can Charlie walk me home?" I asked hopefully.

"Yes, I'd insist," Lucia said.

I lumbered off the hospital bed and walked over to Charlie.

"Charlie," I said gently as I tapped his shoulder.

He bolted straight up and let out a surprised squeak. He had been lost in thought.

"Veri!" he said with a gasp.

"*You* need to walk me home. Doctors' orders," I said, helping him to his feet.

"Veronica," Dr. Weathers called after us, "we will want to see you tomorrow."

"Okay!" I called over my shoulder.

We heard the *beep-beep-beep* of the lab door closing behind us.

"What the heck were you two doing in there?" Nick was standing with the fridge door open. He had been drinking straight from an orange juice container.

"What are you doing not using a glass?" Charlie countered. "That's some serious cooties there."

"I just wanted to see the lab," I cut in.

"Yeah, but the mums were in there so we got chucked out right quick," Charlie said.

"But I've been watching TV for the past hour," Nick said, pointing to the couch. He was watching the classic-film channel.

"Man! The *Thin Man* marathon is on, Charlie! We're missing it!" I exclaimed, spotting one of my favorite films on the screen.

"Oh yeah?" Nick looked impressed. "You like *The Thin Man*?"

"Yes! I shoulda named my dog Asta! They look alike," I answered.

Charlie had taken this opportunity to guide me toward the front door without any more questioning from his older brother.

"Bye, Nick!" Charlie called, slamming the door behind us.

I waited until we were half a block away.

"So?! 'Modified sleep state'? What is that?"

Charlie shrugged. "I don't know how they can deduce anything from a little blood and a lot of green goo."

"Well," I said, trying to look on the bright side, "I guess we'll see what happens. Maybe the powers are going away. Wouldn't that be great?"

"Do you feel any different?" Charlie asked.

"No. I feel the same," I said as we walked up the path to my front door.

My dad's "cooking music" blared from the kitchen.

"Dinner?" I asked Charlie.

His eyes lit up. "Thought you'd never ask."

Charlie wasn't our only dinner guest. Ms. Watson was also in the kitchen, chopping a tomato.

"Hey, Ms. Watson," Charlie greeted her, then gave me the side-eye. "I didn't know you were coming to dinner."

"Funny," Dad butted in, "I didn't know *you* were coming to dinner, Chuck."

"I live to surprise!" Charlie said.

Dad gave Charlie a high five.

"Kiddo," Dad said, giving me a kiss on the head.

I hadn't said anything yet, and neither had Ms. Watson. We were just sort of staring at each other. I felt like all that wet cement in my head was starting to slop around. Someone had turned the mixing truck on and things were starting to work again.

"Do you need any help?" I managed, remembering the stinky death promise I'd made to Dad.

"Nah, we got it," Dad said, and smiled at me. "You look pooped. Why don't you guys head out back?"

"Ooh! Dining alfresco!" Charlie tittered.

"Actually, Chuck, take these," Dad ordered, loading Charlie's arms up with dinner plates. "Set the table while you're out there."

Outside, Charlie and I did just that, but both of us had our eyes glued on the view through the bay window into the kitchen.

"What is going on?" Charlie wondered aloud while he slid a paper napkin under a fork.

I shook my head in similar confusion. Ms. Watson and my dad were in our kitchen making us dinner. Smiling.

"They look very . . . domestic," Charlie observed.

"No," I said.

Charlie stood next to me. I realized I had been holding the same plate for at least a minute.

"It wouldn't be *that* bad, would it?" he asked.

"Yes," I answered.

"He looks . . . happy," Charlie said. "If they are dating—"

"They aren't dating," I said, correcting him.

"But if they are, it's not like it's the end of the world," he reassured me with a nudge.

"They aren't dating."

And just like that, I saw my father put his hand on the small of Ms. Watson's back (*eew*), then she looked up at him and smiled (!!!), and then (deep breath) they kissed.

"Aww," Charlie said.

I covered my face with my hands. "Noooo! They *are* dating."

Dinner? Yeah. Definitely awkward. Not that the lovebirds seemed to notice. I just about threw up on my penne alla pesto. It was pretty obvious that they thought they were keeping all of this under wraps. There weren't any PDAs, thankfully, at the dinner table, but they were both so jolly it was hard to believe they thought they were fooling anyone.

I still wasn't sure in what kind of world something like this would happen. I didn't expect my dad to stay single for the rest of his life, but I didn't expect . . . this. Until six months ago, he loathed this woman, who had tried to bust him for years and years for having secret superpowers.

I felt Charlie's toe jab into my shin.

"Friday? Premiere?" Dad repeated to me.

"Uh, yeah," I said. "Hopefully we'll be done with the movie by then."

"We will!" Charlie chirped. "Wait until you see the monster costume, Rik. Out-bloody-standing. Veri's outdone herself."

"My kid has an eye—what can I say?" Dad beamed at me.

"Thanks," I said, trying to force a smile.

"She's very creative, like her father," Ms. Watson declared, giving my dad a look that, for Watson, was very wistful.

I was totally grossed out. My skin was starting to crawl. Literally, I could see little waves and bumps of flesh slowly crawling down my arm. I covered it with my hand.

Ms. Watson stood up suddenly. "Whoa," she said, with a visible shiver.

"You all right?" Dad asked.

"Just got a rather large shiver down my arms," Ms. Watson said, collecting herself.

I looked at Charlie. Then I realized he had no idea what had just happened to me.

"Uh, Dad, is there any more penne?" I asked as I shoved down what was left on my plate.

"You kiddin' me? We're eating this for the next week," he answered.

Knowing his internal Man of the House would kick in, I stood up to go get my own pasta.

"Sit, sit, sit," Dad instructed as he stood up and grabbed my plate. "I'll get it. Anyone else need anything?"

Charlie raised his hand.

"Except for Chuck?" Rik added, winking at Ms. Watson as he walked away.

I only had to stare at her for three seconds straight before she made an excuse to leave.

"I'm just going to check my phone . . . ," she told Charlie and me as she stood up.

Once we were alone, I grabbed Charlie's elbow to make him focus on me instead of the meal.

"Charlie, the weirdest thing just happened," I said as quietly as I could.

"You stared down a former government agent and she cracked?" he said, and smirked. "Pretty cool."

"No, well, yes, but here's the thing—the skin on my arm was crawling from my powers just when Ms. Watson got her big shiver." I looked at him, expecting a big reaction.

Nothing.

"Do you think it means something?" I asked.

"*Oh!*" He finally grasped it. "You mean, did you *make* Ms. Watson get the heebie-jeebies?"

"Yes!" I hissed.

"But that's not how your powers work," he said very matter-of-factly.

"Dude, we don't know how my powers work," I reminded him.

"Well, yeah, but usually they don't mess with other people," he explained.

He was right, but then something occurred to me. I could see Dad and Ms. Watson coming back, so I had to hurry.

"What if I made you go to sleep earlier?" I asked very quickly.

"What?"

"When you told me to relax—but instead you relaxed so much you fell asleep?" I said.

Charlie frowned, then said, "Data processing," in his best robot voice.

Dad and Ms. Watson came outside. I could tell by the look on Charlie's face that he was still putting the pieces together. Apparently, Dad could tell, too.

"What'd we miss?" Dad asked, giving Charlie a quizzical look.

Charlie lit up, his brain finished calculating.

"This changes everything!" he shouted.

Dad had to go work at the club right after dinner, so I didn't get a chance to question his life choices.

"See ya in the a.m." Dad gave me a hug as he and Ms. Watson headed out the front door.

"Sayonara, Rik!" Charlie waved.

Ms. Watson paused. "Is Weathers staying here? With no additional adult supervision?" she asked Dad.

"Yes," I answered for him. "Charlie hangs out here all the time."

"It's cool," Dad reassured her. "They're good kids."

"Verified," Charlie agreed.

"This is not an ideal situation," Ms. Watson said to Dad.

"Welcome to parenthood," he joked as he shut the door behind them.

Ms. Watson watched us over her shoulder as they walked away. Charlie and I smiled and waved at her.

"This is terrible," I said to him, smile still plastered on my face.

"It won't last," he consoled me. "They're total opposites."

"Opposites attract," I reminded him.

"Forgot about that," he said. "Let's focus on other things, shall we?"

"Good idea," I agreed. "So, I think I made you fall asleep and I think I made Ms. Watson's skin crawl."

"At the lab, you also said that you'd hit her with little lightning bolts," he added.

"True." I pondered for a moment. "But that was just like my other powers. I didn't even notice it being any different. I mean, these things today were like *transfers* of my powers onto other people."

We agreed that a test of our own was in order. We went back outside, just in case things backfired, because Charlie had a very specific request.

"I wanna breathe fire. Veri, I wanna breathe fire. Can you make me breathe fire?" he begged.

"I don't know, Charlie," I said, laughing. He and Einstein were bouncing around like two playful puppies, even though only one of them was actually a playful puppy.

"I have to get really, really mad to breathe fire, and I'm not feeling very mad right now."

"I can make you mad!" Charlie said proudly.

It was late enough, and all of my neighbors' lights were out; they were asleep. It was a low-risk situation.

"Let's give it a try," I said decisively.

"Okay. Okay. Things that make you mad," he said, racking his brain. "Mornings? Pop quizzes? People who walk really slow!"

"All true, buddy, but I think we need something a little deeper."

"Betsy makes you mad."

"Sure does," I answered, "but I think we need to focus on you. If this is what we think it is, I don't want Betsy to be across town breathing fire."

"Oh yeah. Good point," Charlie agreed. "This should be pretty easy, then. I irritate you all the time!"

"What were some doozies?" I asked.

"Hmm . . ." Charlie pondered. "What about the time I *accidentally* made your American Girl doll the test pilot of my homemade spaceship?"

"There's no way that was an accident," I said, remembering the plastic carnage.

"Oh! And what about the time I called your dad and *accidentally* told him that you were out getting your ears pierced."

"Which is the reason I still don't have pierced ears." I grunted. Now I was getting properly mad.

"It was very unhygienic, Veri," he said. "A 'friend of Ted' should not be trusted to stick needles in your head."

"Wait, wait, wait," I said, my brain putting the pieces together. "You thought it was a bad idea and 'accidentally' told my dad? You told him on purpose?"

And with that realization, I was livid. I could feel the powers activating. My throat started to burn and I knew flames were coming. I opened my mouth to let them out, but all that emerged was a puff of smoke.

"What the?" I muttered.

"*Oof*," Charlie said, rubbing his chest. "Penne alla heartbur—"

But before he could get out the *n*, he burped a small flame! It illuminated Charlie's surprised face.

"Ahh!" we screamed in unison once the flame blew out.

"That was amazing! And terrifying and weird, but amazing!" Charlie declared. He celebrated with a cartwheel.

"Oh boy," I said to myself.

"How did you do that?!" Charlie marveled.

"I don't know." I thought about it for a minute. "I guess I was feeling angry *toward* you, and somehow my power went to you." I scratched my head. "Did you feel angry?"

Charlie shrugged. "I guess? I mean, I was pretty distracted by the intense burning sensation."

The ramifications of a new stupidpower problem was definitely not what I wanted to deal with right now. If my powers were spreading to other people, there would be no way to keep them secret anymore.

I didn't want to think about it too much. Suddenly, I just wanted to go to sleep and pretend today never happened.

"It-it could just be a fluke, you know?" I said, trying to calm myself down.

"But—"

"Let's not get ahead of ourselves," I said sharply. "I think we both need a good night's rest. Yeah?"

I didn't wait for Charlie's reply. I waved at him over my shoulder as I went back inside. "See you tomorrow, Charlie. Maybe around ten a.m.?"

"Veri, let's figure this out!" he called after me, but I didn't look back.

Once I had crawled into bed with Einstein, it became

apparent that it was going to be a long night. My brain didn't want to sleep. And for good reason. What was going on with my powers? If other people could feel my powers, how long until my secret got out? I tossed and turned until I heard Dad come home at two thirty a.m. He was singing softly to himself. Sounded like a Sinatra song.

He was happy.

Why did he have to be so happy?

CHAPTER EIGHT
HEART FAILURE

Morning came and I had managed to whip myself into a total frenzy. I had decided that if I never left my room again, I'd never have to deal with any of these stupidpowers or stupid feelings ever again. Dad had knocked on my door twice. I only opened it once to retrieve the orange juice he brought me.

"Just working on the movie," I lied.

"Baby Spielberg killing it," he declared.

"Huh, yeah." I faked enthusiasm.

In reality, I had spent the whole morning convincing myself that the power transfer Charlie and I had experienced wasn't real. That it was, in fact, a fluke. I looked at the clock—10:37 a.m. Like our brains were melded, Charlie texted, wondering where I was. I texted him back that I was too busy to come over and that I'd see him tomorrow. Then I put my phone on silent and shoved it under my mattress as I climbed back into bed.

An hour later, the frequent buzzing had gotten to me. At that point, it was much easier to just go to Charlie's and face the music than read the novel he had texted me.

Dad was napping with a baseball game on TV. I left him a note saying I was at Charlie's if he needed me. Not that he would now that he had Ms. Watson. (I didn't include that last part in my note.)

Nick opened the front door at the Weatherses' for me.

"Hey!" he said, holding the door open. "Big week coming up. You rested and ready?"

"I hope so," I answered. It was the most honest thing I'd said all day.

"You are, don't worry." He leaned against the back of the sofa while I put my backpack down in the entryway. "What's in there?"

"Oh, just my sketchbooks and stuff. Never know when inspiration is going to hit," I said. Then I realized that might have sounded dumb. I felt my nose crinkle.

"I've said it before, and I'm sure I'll say it again: You're a natural, Veri," Nick told me, running his hand through his hair.

I looked down at my feet to hide my face. I knew I was blushing like crazy and definitely did not want to have a stupidpower freak-out here and now. "Thanks," I mumbled.

"Well, it's true," Nick replied in a similar mumbly fashion. Something about his response didn't sound right to me, so, despite my pink cheeks, I looked up. Nick was blushing! Majorly blushing and looking at his feet. I whipped my head around and looked in the hallway mirror. There I was, not a hint of pink in my face at all! I looked back at Nick only to spot some other familiar faces, if you can call them that: two adorable giggling hearts had appeared just behind Nick, over his head.

I couldn't speak. I had transferred my crushing stupid-power onto Nick!

"Veri? That you?" Charlie called from upstairs. His light footsteps made a soft *dub-dub* sound on the hardwood as he left his bedroom.

I needed to get rid of those hearts before Charlie saw them, which would possibly be the most embarrassing thing in the whole wide world.

My panic seemed to reset my powers and I could tell Nick was coming out of it, too. He shook his head and I took the opportunity to cross over behind him and swat at the hearts. They evaded my swings and headed toward the kitchen with a gleeful "*Whee!*"

"Did you hear that?" Nick asked, following after me.

I had the hearts cornered in the kitchen, but with Charlie and Nick about to walk in on us, I didn't know what to do.

"Veri, you *are* here!" Charlie said as he entered the room, with Nick behind.

In desperation, I opened the freezer door to block their view of the hearts. Drawn by the pull of the freezer fan, the hearts moved in closer.

"Oh, uh, hey," I said, trying to keep an eye on my prisoners.

Charlie pressed the button on the house intercom, which piped into the lab. "Veri's here," he said, then let go of the button. "They'll be so happy."

"You're hanging out with my moms?" Nick asked.

"Just, um, trying to get my science skills up for next year," I said, shooting for a plausible explanation.

"Yeah, Veri sucks at science. And that is totally true," Charlie added.

"Hey," I grumbled, annoyed at the subtle insult. But more important, I was about to be surrounded by other inquisitive Weathers family members. I needed to get rid of these hearts.

Beep-beep-beep.

The lab door was about to open behind me, so I did what I had to do.

Slam! (Pop-pop! Yaaaay!)

I popped the hearts by slamming the freezer door on them.

Charlie looked back into the living room, thinking the sound was coming from the TV.

"Veronica!" Lucia cheerfully called to me from the open lab door.

Charlie and I rushed in, but not before I stole a quick glance at Nick. Was he looking at me, too?

Back in the lab and on my hospital bed, Charlie and I tried to explain what had happened the night before.

"It doesn't matter," Dr. Weathers said.

"Doesn't matter?" Charlie asked.

"We need to re-create it in the lab, is what she means," Lucia said. "We need to have it happen here so we don't have to rule out other sources and influences."

"Ah . . . ," I said. I think I understood.

"We can do that! Easy!" Charlie smiled widely at me. "Ready to get mad at your old pal Charlie again?"

I nodded my agreement.

"Okay," Charlie said. He stood and waved his arms dramatically. "Ear piercing!"

Dr. Weathers and Lucia shared a confused look, but instead of explaining, I closed my eyes and tried to recapture my anger from last night. Thing was, I couldn't stop picturing Nick blushing.

"Feeling anything?" Charlie asked.

"Not angry enough," I said.

"Um, okay. We can work with that, I can think of other things." He paused for a moment before saying, "Remember the time you wanted to go see that animated movie about the robots, but I told you it had already left theaters?"

"Yeah?" I opened one eye to look at him.

"It hadn't gone yet."

"Charlie!" I felt a flare of annoyance.

"You know I can't handle sad robots! It's too real!" he explained.

Before I could get my annoyance to upgrade to anger we were interrupted.

Ziii-zii! The buzz of the intercom distracted me. Then Nick's voice totally blew any chance I had of being angry.

"There's a delivery here. Says they need one of your signatures," Nick said. "The box has a giant biohazard symbol on it, so I'm not touching it."

I giggled a little, and I think Lucia noticed.

"It doesn't make sense," Charlie mused as Dr. Weathers went out to collect her package.

It *did* make sense to me, but I couldn't tell them why. It was too embarrassing. *Oh, hey, everybody, I probably can't do this because I can't stop thinking about Nick. Pretty sure I have a crush on him and my powers made him crush on me for about five seconds.*

Nope. Not happening.

"Sorry, everybody," I said quietly.

"Nothing to be sorry about," Lucia comforted me. "Has anything like this power transfer ever happened before?"

I thought about it for a minute. "Well, I guess when I

wiped everyone's memory of me at the dance. That was kind of a power transfer."

"A pretty huge power transfer," Charlie agreed.

"So maybe this is just residual stuff from that?" I wondered.

"Yeah," Charlie said, scratching his head. "Like a glitch."

Lucia nodded. She seemed to be contemplating the idea. "Possibly, but until we have hard data and the event re-created in the lab, it's still a very loose theory."

After Dr. Weathers returned with the box, Lucia took my vitals and strapped a blood pressure cuff on me. "Narrowing things down is all part of the scientific process. Don't fret."

I was fretting. One hundred percent fretting. Maybe deep down inside Nick did like me and the stupidpowers just brought it to the surface? But then why were the hearts there? Those were *my* hearts.

"She's fine," Lucia confirmed, taking off her stethoscope.

"An anomaly," Dr. Weathers said, and wrote something in her tablet before going back to unpacking the biohazard box.

Fine? A girl could dream. "So, what's next?" I asked, eager to figure *something*, anything, out.

"Charlie didn't tell you? Since Nick is here to hold down the fort, we are going away for a few days. For our anniversary." Lucia smiled.

"Going away? I thought I was, you know, top priority." I fumbled. "I'm kinda a mess!"

"We need to formulate more ideas, Veronica," Dr. Weathers explained. "It doesn't matter if we do that here in the lab or on a beach in Miami."

"*Or* a staycation right here in town," Lucia playfully corrected her wife.

I must have looked as gutted as I felt.

"It's only a few days, honey," Lucia consoled me. "We'll still be here if you really need us."

"For emergencies only," Dr. Weathers clarified.

I was completely speechless. Didn't they realize the damage I could do in just a few days?

CHAPTER NINE
LOCO CELEBRITY

I had arrived at camp that morning ready to work. It seemed like the absolute best distraction from whatever was going on with my powers. After the fiasco at Charlie's the day before, I had gone home and read up on some famous directors and how they "ran" their sets. I was nervous, of course; who wouldn't be! I was in charge of the whole thing now, and I really didn't want to let anyone down. And, truthfully, there was another reason to be nervous—Nick. I'd managed to avoid him so far. I was still feeling embarrassed about yesterday, and I had no clue if he remembered it, let alone how he felt. There was no way he could *really* have a crush on me, too. It was just my powers. Had to be.

Anyway, I needed a distraction and boy-oh-boy was I about to get one.

"Veronica, this is our current marketing piece," Rashida said quietly as she covered the microphone of the phone she was talking on. She pinned the phone to her ear with her shoulder and rifled through her bag. After removing her spare phone, tablet, and laptop, she handed me a copy of one of the posters I'd drawn to advertise the movie, all while continuing her phone conversation. Excited, I leafed through the pages. Except it wasn't at all what I had intended. Rashida had Photoshopped in big block letters that said, *Thrills! Chills! And Romance!*

"Romance?" I asked her. Our movie didn't have any romance whatsoever.

She held up one finger, implying I wait for a moment. "Roger that, doll!" She then looked at me and said, "What were you saying?"

"This says 'romance.' We don't have romance in this film."

"Uh-huh," she answered, half listening. She was typing a text message. "We want to get everyone to come see it, right?" she asked.

"Well, yeah," I explained, "but we can't lie to people.

We can't have them expect to see romance and end up with a slimy monster."

"They'll still like it."

"But it's *not* a romance," I told her.

"To *you*," she said.

Touché! I was about to tell her how this could be a slippery slope into false advertising, but I was interrupted by Ted, who was carrying a large bolt of long neon-green faux fur.

"Veronica, Max needs to know how big Avery's head is in order to finish the costume."

I stared at him blankly.

"Avery might be a better source for that information," I suggested.

"Oh yeah!" Ted said like the thought had never occurred to him. He turned to look for Avery.

"Wait, Ted, what's the fabric for?" I asked.

Ted smiled. "Max has been reimagining the costume. That man is on fire!"

None of these words worked for me. "Take me to him."

"What about the romance?" Rashida asked. She sounded a little sad, like I had forgotten her. (I had.)

"Just—just fix it." I added, "I know you'll make it great."

She lit up. "Okay! I'm just about to start our social media campaign. I'm really excited about it!"

"Cool," I said nervously as I followed Ted. Please, *please* let it be cool.

I spotted Max (mainly because of his hat du jour, which looked like a wedge of cheddar cheese) and his "reimagining." I had the feeling that things would never ever, ever be cool ever again. Ted's bolt of horrendous fabric was apparently only a refill for the copious amount that Max had already used. But not just neon green, no—things couldn't be that monochromatic. He had also employed several hundred purple and red sequins. It was like he had taken our original costume and hit it with a magic wand. A wand that made things tacky. And not at all magical.

"Max," I heard myself whisper.

He turned to me, smiling ear to ear. "What do you think?" He proceeded to show me his new mock-up for Hun Su's costume as Jessie. What had been a casual T-shirt and jeans was now a pink jumpsuit with multiple utility pockets.

"She's speechless!" Ted congratulated Max.

"Oh, wait. It gets better!" Max said. He turned the jumpsuit around so I could see the back. He had painted a unicorn on it that had a rainbow beam shooting from its horn and a *J* painted on its left flank.

I couldn't believe it. Max had taken what we had agreed on—my sketches of what the characters should look like—and had done the complete opposite. He had gone so far as to redo a costume we had already made! The River Monster costume had been a lot of hard work, involving more than a few hot-glue burns. We had suffered for it and now it was a shell of what it had been. A shiny, technicolor shell.

"No . . . ," I squeaked.

Max furrowed his brow. "Excuse me?"

"This isn't what we planned. Why are they so different from the sketches?" I asked as nicely as I could. I didn't want to seem like a jerk or make him think his work wasn't good—it was good, just nothing at all like what we needed.

"You mean, what *you* planned?" he asked. "I'm the costumer. I deserve to have my artistic input, too."

"Why didn't you say something before?" I asked. "Like when we were making the monster costume?"

"I tried! You and Charlie were too busy having your giggle-fest to hear anything I said."

"What?" I was dumbstruck. I had zero memory of this.

"These are better. Period," Max said.

"No. These are amazing, but they aren't right for the movie."

"I'm not making anything else. You're going to have to get over it."

I looked around for backup but didn't see Ellie. Then I spotted Nick working with the Tech Twins. I wasn't ready to face him. Max must have noticed.

"Or you could tell Nick and have him realize that you have no control on your own set," he said. "Might be a bummer for him to know he picked the wrong person for director."

I wanted to shove all the sequins in the world down Max's throat.

"How can we compromise?" I asked him through gritted teeth.

"We can't," he said flatly.

I was getting really agitated with Max. I felt like he had

intentionally tricked me and was now rubbing it in my face. Somehow he thought he had gotten the upper hand. I was trying to keep my cool, but I could feel my irritation starting to eat away at me, and it was bordering on stupidpowers. Then it tripped over the border. Suddenly maniacal moths were nibbling away at Max's jeans and, thankfully, all his new costumes! "Ahh!" Max screeched, shaking out every piece of fabric in sight. Ted helped him by fanning the costumes with his straw cowboy hat.

I gently swiped a few fingers through the air and let out a half-hearted, "Shoo."

Nick had noticed the commotion and came jogging over to us. Seeing him caught me off guard and must have broken my power transfer link to Max. As quickly as the moths appeared, they disappeared. At least they weren't as persistent as the hearts.

"Whoa, what's going on?" Nick asked, observing the scene. Max had climbed on top of a table and was holding the pink jumpsuit. Both his pants and the legs of the jumpsuit had been munched all the way up to the knees.

"Killer bugs!" Max cried.

"Those were mental," Ted agreed.

"Just moths," I explained to Nick, but I didn't look up at him.

"Sorry, guys," Nick consoled us as he looked for damage on the new monster costume. "Do you think we have time to fix it, Veri?"

I forced myself to look at him and instantly had to keep myself from bursting out laughing. He had his back turned toward Max and Ted and was giving me a wide-eyed "these costumes are insane" look.

"I'm sure our costumer can fix them right up," I said. I felt my face contort into what I was hoping was a look that told him how much I loathed these costumes.

"I know you guys have it under control," Nick said, patting my shoulder. He was about to go back to the Tech Twins when Max let out a gasp.

Heads turned toward the road and an impressed murmur spread through our small ranks.

It was a white stretch limousine. I had never seen one in real life. The closest place they could even be rented was over an hour away! It pulled up to the curb and the driver, who was wearing a uniform with a cap that looked like one a pilot might wear, hopped out and rushed to a door in the rear. He gracefully opened the door and stood behind it, waiting for his passenger to exit. A few seconds later, a man emerged. He was tall and rather round, his age was somewhat indeterminable—older than thirty, younger than sixty—and he was wearing a blazer with a T-shirt and jeans. Before taking in the view, he lowered his sunglasses down from his forehead.

"Quaint," he said to no one in particular.

Mr. Stephens came bursting out of the theater.

"Mr. Aldicott!" Mr. Stephens sang as he rushed to the stranger's side.

"Call me Clem," the man replied slyly.

Mr. Stephens looked like he might burst with joy. "Okay, *Clem.*"

A stream of theater actors followed Mr. Stephens, and now they were all in the front yard of the theater, smiling shyly and meeting the mystery man.

"What's this nonsense?" Charlie asked, joining me.

"I wish I knew," I replied.

"'Ang on," Charlie said, his fake accent even thicker than usual. "That's Tony Steel!"

I shrugged my shoulders at Charlie. I had no clue who this guy was.

"He said his name was Clem," I said.

"Charlie!" Nick tittered as he jogged up to us.

"Tony Steel!" they exclaimed in unison.

"Guys?" I said.

"Tony Steel was a character on our absolute favorite TV show growing up," Nick explained.

"*Steel Roses*!" Charlie marveled at my blank expression. "You never watched *Steel Roses* with us?!"

"Oh!" My brain churned. "The one about the undercover cop 'working' at a flower shop that was the hub of all crime in that city?"

"Yes!" they said again, in unison.

"Ah," was my bland reply.

"We have to meet him," Charlie said to Nick, who was already nodding in agreement.

I followed the giddy boys toward Mr. Stephens and his troupe. What was an actual actor doing here in our tiny town? This couldn't be good.

"This can't be good," Ellie echoed my thoughts as she stood with me, watching the boys shake hands with their slick-haired hero. I wondered if his hair was real, which made me even more aware of Ellie's magical mane, which had washed out to a pastel blue. She had pulled it into a high bun and wrapped it with a sparkly hair tie that had strands of sequins hanging from it.

"Your hair is gorgeous today," I had to tell her.

"Thanks!" She added, "You have the coolest hair I've ever seen. I'd kill for that volume."

My heart fluttered in my chest.

"Attention, everyone!" Mr. Stephens interrupted our hair-love party. "I thought you *all* should know," he said, looking directly at us campers, "we have added a new cast member. Star of stage and screen, Clem Aldicott, has agreed to join our production as the multifaceted Captain Hook!"

Clem Aldicott flashed his whiter-than-humanly possible teeth and waved at us, like we had been waiting for him all day, his adoring fans.

Mr. Stephens put his arm around Clem Aldicott's doughy shoulders. "Let's get you into the theater, shall we?" As he passed by Nick and Charlie he added, "So much for your premiere. *Everyone* will be dying to see a real celebrity."

"That guy just keeps getting worse," Ellie said.

"Full of surprises," Betsy chimed in. She had filmed the whole thing from behind us. "He's an enigma of awful."

Ellie laughed, and Betsy actually smiled. She SMILED.

The hubbub died down once all the theater folk went back into their hive and the scraggly film folks were left out in the cold. Suddenly I felt as if we looked like idiots. Nick's expression made me think he had the same notion, though he quickly wiped away all traces of it.

"Back to work, everybody," he said too cheerily. I guessed he was overcompensating for his true feelings.

We all trudged back to our positions. The tone had definitely changed. With the theater's addition of a professional actor, what chance did we have? If I was being completely honest, which I knew I could only be with myself—I was trying to be a real director—I would say that we were kinda screwed. A real actor had never set foot in Pearce, and surely the townsfolk would much rather see him than the same kids they see every day. Especially when those kids were supposed to be terrifying but are instead covered in sequins and unicorns.

"Hey, everyone, take five," I directed. I needed the break more than anyone, I think.

I took respite under a gangly willow behind the theater, next to the river. One side was covered with moss and had the most luscious grass under it. I sat there, pulling my knees up to my chest. Here I was invisible, but not actually invisible, which for me was the absolute best. In my world, where I could become invisible without meaning to, even this sad moment was a relief. I mean, who knew so many emotions could exist at the same time, right? Being sad and annoyed about Clem Aldicott, but also being happy about being sad because it was so normal. Growing up is freaking weird.

Anyway, my moment of solitude was just that. A moment. Fleeting.

"Are *you* the weeping willow?" Charlie joked, sitting next to me under the dangling branches.

"Who's to say?" I joked back. "Don't give my stupid-powers any ideas, pal!"

Then it got quiet. The kind of quiet that would be really uncomfortable if it was with anyone you didn't know that well. Since I was with Charlie, I knew that a highly honest conversation was about to happen.

"You freaking out?" he asked quietly.

"Little bit," I confessed.

"This isn't on you, Veri."

"It's not? I'm the director."

"I get it, but remember, it's *our* movie. All of us. You aren't the only one who's responsible," he reminded me.

"It feels like I'm the only one who really cares about this making sense and being a scary movie."

"Hey!" Charlie protested.

"I mean, other than you, obviously." I yanked at my purple shoelaces.

"What? You don't see the endless dedication in those three?" he pointed at Avery, Rashida, and Max, who had taken this short break as an open invitation to start playing their Magic card game.

"Ugh."

"I'm not gonna lie, the fact that the playhouse has Clem Aldicott is pretty amazing. If we could have someone like that in our movie . . . Too bad he's the first, and probably last, TV star to come here," Charlie confessed.

"He's the only star within the next thousand miles," I said. The wheels were starting to turn in my brain. I had a big idea. "And we have him right next door."

CHAPTER TEN
PREMIERE-ADONNA

Directors seize every opportunity they are given. And I had spent the whole morning with one eye on the theater, waiting for my moment. Hence me running over like an Olympic sprinter the instant I spotted Clem Aldicott sunning himself on the front steps.

"Morning," I said to him.

He lazily turned to look at me, a forced smile on his lips. "Darling, he said, 'take fifteen,' and I intend to take a full fifteen."

"Oh, I don't—I'm not in the play, I'm working on the movie. Over there." I pointed to Betsy and the Tech

Twins, who were attempting to attach a spotlight to a stepladder.

"Really?" he said. His tone changed completely. He sat up straight and pushed his sunglasses onto the top of his head, suddenly giving me his full attention and smiling genuinely.

"Yes!" I was thrilled that he seemed so eager to talk to me, but . . . "I mean, it's our summer camp film—obviously, we're just kids."

"Nonsense," he said, shaking his head. "Film is where it's at. With the YouTubes and the internet, who knows, your film could be the next big player at Sundance."

I liked how this dude thought.

"So, you aren't only interested in theater?" I asked, trying not to seem too hopeful.

"Heavens no," he answered. "I'm playing these small-town theaters to put bread on the table. I'd gnaw off my right arm to see my name on the big screen again."

He looked wistfully into the distance. It was so intense that I became sure he was looking at something. Perhaps the spirit of a long-lost love had returned from the grave and was wafting in the sky somewhere over the courthouse.

But when I followed his gaze, there was nada. Man, he really was an actual actor.

"I'm Veronica, the director."

"*Très chic!* Female directors are all the rage," he mused.

"Uh, yeah. Mr. Aldicott—"

"Call me Clem, Director Veronica," he bellowed.

"Okeydokey." I wondered if I was ever going to finish my thought. "Well, I know you are super busy, but we'd love to have you do a cameo in—"

"Certainly!" he interrupted.

There you go.

"Just to be completely clear, we can't pay you anything," I said.

"Back end?" he asked like I knew what he was talking about.

"Yes?"

"Perfect. Sundance here we come!" he exclaimed, thrusting both fists into the air.

Clem couldn't work us into his rehearsal schedule until Thursday. We had hoped to finish our final shots and start editing the movie by then, but sometimes you have to work extra hard to make something impressive. Having Clem Aldicott in your first film is pretty impressive.

Even more impressive were everyone's reactions to me snagging Clem! It was like they finally had some respect for me.

"Not too bad, Veronica," Max said.

"Thanks," I said, trying not to cringe as he wrapped a feather boa around Hun Su's neck.

Rashida smiled. "We might show up Mr. Stephens after all."

Avery nodded in silent agreement.

"Showing up Mr. Stephens or not," Nick interjected, "it'll be fantastic for all of you to have a movie with a professional actor on your reel."

"Exactly what I was thinking," I said. "And on our very first movie."

"Smooth sailing, then!" Max cheered.

"Well, that means we need to work overtime today and tomorrow to film everything, so that we can start editing ASAP," I warned them. I could feel this was starting to swing in a way I wasn't expecting.

"We've got this, Veronica," Max said gruffly. Now that

Betsy was off my case, Max was quickly filling her shoes. "You don't have to be a dictator about it."

"Excuse me?" Charlie said, jumping to my defense.

Be cool, Veronica. Be a pro, I told myself.

"Let's get to work," I said, ignoring Max.

And that we did. But what it really felt like was that my fellow film students were only working on making everything super-duper hard.

Our silent monster, Avery, seemed to be afraid of being seen. Every time I would call action, he'd instantly lose his confidence.

"Avery, just remember: You are a monster! You have all the power!" I said, trying to give him his motivation. "As far as you are concerned, this land has been stolen from you."

Avery stretched out his arms in a sheepish, mummy-like walking position. A muffled *"Grrrr"* came from his mask. Betsy was beside me, filming it all. I heard her snicker.

"Not funny," I said.

"So funny," she said.

"Does it look any better on camera?" I asked her.

"Define 'better,'" she answered.

That wasn't good. That wasn't good at all.

We tried what felt like a million more times but couldn't get Avery to be scary. The constantly changing lights from the Tech Twins didn't help, either. They were having endless arguments about what color lights to use and instead of coming to an agreement, they just decided to switch between each of their preferences. When I told them they had to choose one, they looked at me like I had asked them to cut off a limb.

Then Rashida brought me up-to-date on her social media blast. She hadn't cut out the romance bit! But that wasn't the worst of it—she had claimed we were taking donations for charity.

"Why would you say that?" I asked her.

"Because people want to help a good cause," she explained.

"But what cause are we helping?"

"Does it matter? Couldn't we just keep the money?" she genuinely asked. "I mean, we don't have any. We're a good cause."

"No," I said, but I couldn't seem to find any other words. It had been a long, long day and I was starting to feel fried. For all the research I'd done, none of the other directors seemed to have so little say in their own movies.

Every crew had respect for those directors' "vision." Not here. Not for me.

The rest of the day didn't get any better. Which meant our film was getting worse and worse. A single thought kept running through my head:

Had I made a huge mistake?

"Action!" I shouted. For the fifteenth time that day. Who knew it would get old so quickly? Admittedly, I was cranky. Like, really properly cranky. I had hoped that a new day would bring a renewed sense of calm and happiness about our project, but instead I was tired and frustrated and, well, really properly cranky.

Avery clumsily plodded through the waist-high grass by the embankment. He tripped over a log and went rolling down the hill.

"I'm all right!" his muffled voice called from the bottom.

"Cut!" I sighed. This guy was gonna kill me. I knew we should've picked Charlie. I was so annoyed and disgusted with Avery. At this point any decent human would have quit for the sake of the film. *Grr!*

Betsy looked up from the camera. "That guy," she said.

"Yeah," I sputtered before I remembered: "Wait, you were the one who wanted Avery as the monster."

"Well, I was wrong," she said flatly, but earnestly. "We should replace him with Charlie." Then outta nowhere Betsy barked. Like, "*Ruff!*" As in, how a guard dog barks.

"What was that?" I asked. Even though I already knew what was happening.

"Just a cough," she said, rubbing her throat. She turned back around and I could see a swath of dog fur had grown down her neck and back. Her normally short hair was now very coarse and scruffy in the back. I had transferred my stupidpower to Betsy! She was turning into the snarling, angry guard dog that I was feeling like!

Ellie joined us. "Nick is just helping Avery up."

"We want Avery and Charlie to switch roles, Ellie," Betsy said.

"Whoa. Where'd that come from?" she asked, looking at me.

"Betsy changed her mind." I added, "Since Avery is, you

know, putting us way behind schedule and ruining our movie." I felt the same surge of detestation and loathing for Avery rise in me again.

Ellie's nose twitched like she smelled something. Actually, it was more like she was a dog who smelled the trail of something.

"You're right," she surprisingly conceded. "I'll take care of it."

"Excellent," Betsy grunted. Her guard dog temperament was fading.

"Nice hair, by the way, Betsy," Ellie complimented her, as she turned to walk away.

"You, too," Betsy said as we both spotted a rough patch of dog fur on the back of her head.

Crap. My powers had gotten Ellie, too.

"Weirdo?" Betsy said flatly and rolled her eyes at me.

Did we need to have this talk right now? Betsy knew about my powers and hadn't said anything to anyone about them. Yet.

"I can't help it," I explained quietly.

"*Le duh*," Betsy said, then ran her fingers through her hair. She froze when her hands hit the patch of spiky dog hair in the back. "This better not be what I think it is."

"I really, really can't help it! I'm sorry!"

"Don't do it again."

"What did I just tell you? I can't—"

She glared at me.

"I won't. I won't." I wanted to ask her something, but I wasn't sure it was a good idea. "Um, Betsy, not that I'm not extremely grateful, but why haven't you said anything to anyone about my . . . thing?"

She shrugged at me. "What's the point?"

"Oh, uh, ruining my life, I'd guess?"

"And what would that get me?"

"Fair point."

"Besides," she added, "turns out you have a good idea every once in a while."

She walked away, leaving me in total and utter shock. That was a compliment, right?

Disturbingly quickly, Avery handed over the monster suit to Charlie, and our new monster was ready to make his entrance.

"Let's roll!" Charlie said, his voice muffled inside the mask.

But as we continued our shoot, things only got rockier.

"Line!" Hun Su cried out again. She had forgotten pretty much every other line for the past twenty minutes. At one point she even forgot her own character's name. I could only guess it was the feeling of impending doom; we clearly weren't going to finish shooting in time.

"Weirdo, we're losing light." Betsy pointed at the sky, like I somehow could control the sun.

The Tech Twins nodded in solidarity. "Yeah, we think this is pretty pointless," Lizzie said.

Everyone was getting more anxious by the minute. Grumpier.

"Pointless?" I asked, looking around for support from Ellie and Nick, but they were nowhere to be seen.

"They mean, we're never gonna get all the shots we need in time. Especially when someone can't string together two lines," Betsy explained.

"Is that what you think, too?"

She shrugged, "Makes sense."

Unbelievable.

Avery, who was putting on the "Helpless Victim" costume that had been Charlie's, finally decided to speak. And he didn't hold back. "Seriously, I'm starting to think this whole idea was dumb. It's never gonna work. We can't do this. We're just kids!"

His impassioned despair seemed to strike a chord with the other campers.

"Yeah! You're the director, Veronica; you are supposed to make us good!" Dean of the Tech Twins shouted from behind their laptop.

Where in the heck were Ellie and Nick? I needed reinforcements!

"Let's just relax," I told them. "Set up and regroup for the next shot. We can talk about everything when Nick and Ellie get back."

"Whatever," Avery said. "If this movie bombs, it's your fault."

I walked back to my director's chair to grab my water bottle and take a breather.

Maybe they were right. I wanted to be a good director, but it certainly looked like everything was falling apart. And maybe it was good that Nick and Ellie were MIA. I definitely didn't want them to see me sucking so bad.

"Betsy, I think it would be great if we could get this shot from the water," I suggested.

"You mean, get *in* the water?" she asked suspiciously.

"Yeah! It would look awesome!"

"No."

"Why not?"

"I don't do water," she said.

"Any water? Like, no bathing or drinking?" I asked.

"Um, like, nothing where there could be fish. They creep me out." She looked away, then added, "Weirdo."

"*Argh!*" a frustrated voice yelped out. The Tech Twins had spilled a soda on their laptop.

I sighed. "Come on, you two," I muttered to myself.

I left them to sop up their sticky mess while I checked in with Charlie, who was running lines with Hun Su. Bless his heart, he was trying to get her back in character.

"You can't laugh, Hun Su," he practically begged. "You're about to be eaten."

"You're scared," I added, "like, more scared than you've ever been in your life."

"I'm sorry," she said with a snort. "I giggle when I'm nervous."

"Well," I offered, "think of a time you were really scared, and try to use that emotion. Pretend it's happening right now."

"That's a great idea," Charlie agreed.

"I can't," Hun Su moaned, pushing her lips into a pout.

But it is *a great idea*, I said to myself. My power transfer had worked to my advantage earlier—getting Charlie recast as the River Monster. Maybe I should try to actually use it to help Hun Su and get the movie back on track! But was it worth the risk? My powers weren't consistent. Especially with fear. That was a tricky emotion. Sometimes you wanted to run and hide, and sometimes you wanted to attack your fear. How would that manifest in me, and in Hun Su?

I spotted Nick and Ellie walking back across the grass. They were coming from town, and neither looked very happy.

I had to make this work. I had to be brave.

And scared.

There had been a lot of times in the last few years where Hun Su scared me. She didn't scare me like a psycho murderer hiding in the woods or a clown, but she did scare me with her ability to socially annihilate me at any second, which is scarier than any clown.

"Charlie," I said, "keep working with her."

I took a few steps back and closed my eyes until I could barely see anything except for Hun Su. As I tried to concentrate, I couldn't help but be distracted by the Tech Twins arguing about what color lighting was scarier: red or blue. I needed to put all my focus on Hun Su, so I dug through Charlie's backpack (sorry, Charlie!) and borrowed his ginormous headphones. I stuck the plug end into my pocket, so it at least looked like I was listening to something instead of just creeping on Hun Su, which was pretty much what I was really doing.

Now that it was quiet and my vision was focused, I thought back to the spring, when I had just gotten my powers and how, more than once, Hun Su almost caught me in the middle of one. Then the worst possible thing had happened and she saw pictures of me in the middle of some really embarrassing powers! If I hadn't accidentally (whoops!) wiped the memories of everyone at my school, where would I be now? Hun Su could've ended me.

It took a minute for the fear to really rise, but when it did, and I felt the familiar grossness is my stomach, it showed up fiercely in Hun Su! Her posture straightened, her eyes became steely and her lines were now screaming out of her lungs so hard that it sounded like she was hooked up to a sound system!

Charlie whipped his head to look at me, I gave him a

quick thumbs-up, and he clumsily forced his monster mask over his face.

"Betsy, Tech Twins! Action!" I called, and they sprang to it as best they could.

"I will slay you, beast!" Hun Su yelled at Charlie as he ducked to miss one of her blows.

Like the script called for, Charlie lunged toward our hero, but, unlike the script called for, Hun Su kicked Charlie's feet out from under him. He couldn't help but let out an unintentional "*Oaw!*" as he face-planted in the mud. Betsy looked at me, a silent question of whether we should cut or not. I shook my head no.

"Good call," Nick said quietly as he and Ellie joined us. "We can edit that out in postproduction."

Charlie got back up and they continued the scene. He just had to survive a few more lines.

Ellie nudged me. "He always says 'we'll fix it in post,' but we never do."

The distraction was enough for me to break my concentration—and break my connection with Hun Su, who had just delivered the final (and hopefully fake) death stroke to Charlie.

With my powers depleted, she let out an adorable giggle.

"Cut!" I yelled before anyone could spot the difference in her behavior.

Holy crud! I got what I wanted using my powers! Twice! Maybe this movie could be saved after all.

Now I needed to change Max's feelings about psychedelic faux fur. I pulled Charlie aside.

"Can you rip it or something?" I asked, pretending I was going over the script with him.

"Rip what? The costume?" he asked. "I dunno about that—"

A quiet *rip* cut him off. I wasn't up for discussion and had taken matters, or in this case green fur, into my own hands.

"Oh, hey, Max, there seems to be a rip in the monster," I called out, feigning innocence.

Max trotted over and investigated the rip. "Weird place for it to burst," he muttered to himself. Then his eyes lit up. "Oh! I have a fantastic hot dog patch I could use!"

"Hot dog? Why would a river monster have a hot dog patch on him?!" I asked, frenzied.

"Who knows what he'd pick up in the river," Max said.

Lucky for me, I didn't have to work very hard to pull up emotions on Max. He was so in tune with the ebb and flow of opinions in fashion trends that he could easily read my feelings. I just focused on my disgust over everything he'd added to the costume. By the time he returned with his sewing kit, he'd had a change of heart. And by "heart" I mean a completely controlled change of emotions.

"These sequins . . . What was I thinking?" he said to himself with disdain. "Can you give me, like, twenty minutes? This whole thing needs to be reworked."

"Yes!" I said happily.

Max blinked repeatedly; my change of emotion had broken our link. I quickly remembered the hot dog patch. The hot dog patch!

Twenty minutes later, we had a costume that looked exactly like what I had originally wanted. And a promise that Hun Su's costume would be toned down as soon as he could get to it. He assured me that the changes would work "thematically" and wouldn't interfere with the footage we had already shot. I was so happy! Finally things were going my way. And I wasn't about to stop there.

Within the hour, I had "convinced" the Tech Twins to go with natural-seeming lighting and had Rashida plaster all of social media with a scarier, not-romantic version of our poster. If I concentrated hard enough and found the right emotions, every single conversation played out easily and exactly how I wanted it! By the end of the day, my confidence was sky high, even though my emotions were worn out.

Man, was I beat by the time I got home. That was a lot of emotions for one day. I needed a good night's rest and absolutely zero percent drama. Usually that was guaranteed at our house, but since Ms. Watson first crossed our threshold, things had changed. The last time I needed my Dad alone, things didn't go so well. Right before I opened the front door, I asked the universe for a little favor.

"Please don't let Ms. Watson be here. Please don't let Ms. Watson be here."

Behold! She was not there! In fact, home felt like the soothing oasis my battered soul needed at the moment. Lights were low. Music was chill. And Dad was smoking a cigar on the back porch. A sign that all was well. It felt like things were exactly like they should be.

"You look like crap," he joked as I curled up next to him on the palm-print cushion.

I laughed. "I feel like crap!"

"Long day at the office?" he asked.

"Yeah, making movies is hard. I'm due for a quiet night in," I told him.

"Well, good, 'cause I wanna talk to you about something before I head to work at the club. Something important," he said, putting his gigantic hand over mine, covering it completely.

"A-are you okay?" I asked, suddenly very worried.

"Oh, no! No, no. Nothing like that. I'm totally healthy," he assured me. "And I'm really happy."

"Phew," I sighed.

"You see, Veri, I should have told you this a while back, but it seemed crazy and destined to fail at the time, so I didn't want to bug you."

Ugh. He wanted to talk about Ms. Watson.

"You want to tell me that you've been dating Ms. Watson," I offered.

"You knew this whole time?" he puzzled. "Wait, how long have you known?" He paused.

Then *I* paused. Something about the way he said it . . .

"*Wait*, how long have you been dating?" I was starting to feel like I had missed something.

"You first," he instructed, before exhaling a smoke ring.

"How about we both say our answer on three?" I asked, hoping he'd go for it.

He shrugged his agreement.

I counted, "One, two, three . . ."

"Last weekend!" I said proudly.

"Since June," he said, cringing.

"Whoa." I put my hands up. "Did you really just say that?"

"I know—I know it was a jerk move," he admitted. "I shouldn't have kept it from you."

"That's right!" I snapped. "You don't trust me? You don't think I could handle it? You dating that terrifying woman?!" I was getting really riled up.

Dad rolled his eyes and shrugged, defeated. "And you wonder why I thought you couldn't handle it."

"There shouldn't be anything for me to have to 'handle,'" I told him, trying to pull my emotions back in. Spoiler alert: wasn't going to happen. "Y-you are bringing her into our house, Dad. *Our* house! We don't even know if she is actually on our side," I said, realizing this as I was talking.

"Veri—"

"No, Dad, listen! We don't know if she even really left her job—the job to hunt us down. That's bananas!" The things I was saying were making total sense to me. Why weren't we more suspicious of Ms. Watson? Why hadn't we asked for proof that she wasn't going to tell everyone our secret? I was becoming more dubious of my dad's girlfriend (barf) by the second. I wished Dad was, too.

Except . . .

Using my power transfer, I could *make* Dad suspicious of Ms. Watson. It was possibly a bad idea. I mean, playing with Dad's perception was a little messed up. On the other hand, it was for the greater good. We definitely didn't need Ms. Watson in our lives, even if she was on our side.

"This is not open for debate," Dad started to say, but then he slowed down, like a brand-new thought had taken over his mind.

I stared at him, hard and steely, really focusing on how we knew pretty much nothing about Ms. Watson. She could totally be playing us! Dad got a very faraway look in his eye. He seemed a little out of it and definitely like he was thinking. My powers had transferred my emotion! He was getting suspicious of Ms. Watson! I could feel him resisting, though; he was strong. And his familiarity with stupidpowers probably didn't hurt.

Dad's phone buzzed with an incoming call.

"It's her," he said, his eyes narrowing.

I motioned for him to pick it up. For whatever reason, it was really hard to keep my concentration on how suspicious of Ms. Watson I was. I wasn't sure if it was because Dad also had powers or because I was so exhausted from doing this same exact thing all day. Either way, I knew I had to get this done quick before my scheme fell to pieces.

"Hello?" Dad said warily.

There was a pause, then the muffled sounds of Ms. Watson saying something I couldn't quite hear.

"I think she's being smarter about this than I was," Dad said. "She's not sure this is a good idea, and neither am I anymore."

"What?" I heard Ms. Watson reply.

I closed my eyes and thought about how Ms. Watson had lied to everyone about being my guidance counselor just to get close to me.

"We don't really know anything about you," Dad continued, "and who's to say you even have our backs? You might be collecting info on us to get your old job back!"

There was a quiet murmur of something sad from the other side of the line.

"Well, it's what I've decided. Don't call me, and don't come to work tomorrow. I don't think it's right for you to see Veri ever again, either," he said.

Ms. Watson was saying something, but Dad took the phone away from his ear and hung up.

"I don't know what I was thinking, dating that one," he said to me.

I smiled, letting go of my forced feelings. Almost instantly, Dad's face changed again. He looked at his phone like he wasn't sure what had happened.

"Let's go watch TV," I suggested, pulling him up and toward the living room.

"Uh, okay," he said, still perplexed.

We watched TV in virtual silence until I went to bed. Whenever I peeked at Dad he occasionally had this look like he was trying to sort out what happened to him. He had broken up with Ms. Watson, he'd had those feelings, but now he seemed to be questioning them.

Before I headed up to my room, I told him, "I think it

was a good idea to break up with Ms. Watson, Dad. She'd never really understand us anyway."

He nodded. "Night, baby. I'll try not to wake you up when I get back from the club."

"Night," I said quietly. If I was being completely honest, I'd say that Dad looked sad, and that didn't make me feel great about what I had done. I reminded myself that he would get over it. And we were safer this way. Right?

CHAPTER ELEVEN
A SHOCKING TWIST

Bang-bang-bang!

The pounding on the door jolted me out of the deepest sleep I had had in a long time.

"Up! Veri! Now!" Dad grouched through the door.

I looked at the clock; it was only 5:37 a.m. What in the heck was going on?

"Whaaaaaat?" I groaned, but he didn't answer. He had already gone back downstairs.

I half rolled out of bed and dragged myself down the stairs. Dad was sitting at the kitchen table, steam rising from his coffee cup. By the look on his face, I was surprised steam wasn't rising from his head, too.

"What?" I asked. I had seen this look before. Not quite as fierce as it was now, but I had seen it.

"You get on *my* case about keeping things from you, but *you* can just decide to not tell me something this freaking important and it's no big deal to you?" he barked.

This was a delicate situation. A fine line that I needed to walk very, very carefully. At this point, there were a few things he could be mad at me for not telling him. I didn't want to inform him of something that wasn't presently pissing him off. 'Cause the two main things—the experiments and controlling his emotions—were pretty big doozies.

I filled my cheeks up with air and blew out slowly, then said, "Could you elaborate?"

Dad laced his fingers together and stretched his neck, which let out a loud *crack!*

"You, Veronica McGowan, without consulting me, told two adults about your condition. These adults happen to be scientists," he stated.

"Is that it?" I sputtered.

"Is that it?" he gasped.

"You know what I mean."

"No, I don't," he said. "I don't know what you mean. At. All."

"How'd you find out?" I asked.

He leaned on the table, putting the palms of his hands against his eyes. "You know I took a couple extra hours at the club last night for that jazz thing?"

"Yeah?"

"Lucia and Daphne came," he said, "and they were under the impression that I knew."

"I never told them you knew," I clarified.

"Because it is insane that you didn't tell me, Veri. It's basic common sense, something that I thought you had in abundance. Until now."

"Dad, we are talking about superpowers! I don't think this is the realm of common sense," I said defensively.

"Don't," he warned. "Don't even try it with me."

"I'm sorry."

"You're done with those tests," he demanded. "They said they didn't have any findings yet, and guess what? They aren't going to find anything."

"But—" I started. I wanted to tell him why I did it—to keep Charlie here.

He didn't care. "You're gonna tell them that your condition is gone. It just went away."

"You want me to lie to them?"

"Well, after how you lied to me, I'd think you're an expert."

If Dad had a mic, he would have dropped it.

I opened my mouth to say more, but he just pointed up the stairs, telling me the conversation was over.

"Oh, geez," Charlie said as we waited for the last of the campers to arrive. "I should have realized it was their 'date night.' I'm sorry."

"Dad really flew off the handle," I said. "Told me I couldn't let them run tests on me anymore."

"He's just trying to protect you," Charlie added, "not that it helps."

"What are we going to do, Charlie? I mean, if your parents can't do research on me, then you're going to have to move."

"We won't let that happen. We'll think of something."

He was trying to reassure me, but I could tell that he was just as worried as I was.

"And who knows what punishment awaits me tonight," I said.

"You shoulda mind melded him to not be mad at you," Charlie joked.

"I wish I would have thought of it—I was half asleep." I rubbed my tired eyes. "Using my powers on other people is exhausting. I don't know how I'll be able to do it today."

My new pal Clem Aldicott had agreed to play the missing father of our heroine, Jessie. They are reunited at the end of the film after she saves the world. Clem only had two lines, but we were so excited to have a "real" movie star onboard!

"Seriously, Veronica, this is some ninja-like, directorial magic," Nick said in awe, as he passed Charlie and me. We watched from afar as Clem got his makeup done by Betsy.

"Definitely something . . ." Charlie trailed off. He was looking at me like we had a secret. We had many secrets, but I knew what he was thinking—that I'd used my powers to convince Clem to do the movie. But this was the first time in the past few days where I hadn't used my powers to get what I wanted. It felt good.

A few minutes later, Clem was standing in front of the camera and every last camper was watching. Silently waiting for the magic of a *real* actor to bless our movie.

I had been feeling woozy all morning and completely emotionally exhausted. After spending the last couple days trying to shape this movie into something awesome, I was really glad that I wouldn't have to influence Clem to get a good performance. The movie would be better, everyone would be happy, and I would get a little break, thanks to the professional among us.

"Ready when you are, Director Veronica!" Clem's voice swelled as he gave me a wink.

I slipped on my headphones so I could hear the dialogue as it came through the microphone above his head.

"Aaand, action!" I called out for what would be the last time during this shoot.

Clem stepped toward Hun Su as Jessie, a look of true disbelief upon seeing her face.

"Daughter?" he said quietly.

Yes! I thought. *There's a pro, proing it up!*

Unexpectedly, Clem threw his hands up into the air and cried out, "Dauuuuugh-tteeeeer!" at full volume before dropping to his knees and wailing.

Betsy and I looked at each other. Was he kidding? Or did he think this over-the-top craziness was what we wanted? I didn't call "cut." Maybe he was just warming up?

On his hands and knees in the muddy bank, Clem continued, "I thought you were ne'er to return." He crawled over to Hun Su, wrapping his dirty arms around her ankles. "That I should die, alone and with only the bittersweet memory of my child's love!" he called out, shaking one of his hands in the air, then flailing back into the mud and weeping again.

"Cut!" I called out, without even registering I had said it.

Clem stood up, beaming. "I know I went a little off-book there, but I felt it. In the moment, I knew exactly what my character would do." He gave me another wink before accepting a towel from Nick.

I looked around at the other campers, expecting the same look of disbelief Betsy had, but at that very instant, they all started clapping wildly. Clem Aldicott took a minor bow and waved them off, like he was embarrassed. I had to do something.

"Uh, Clem, that was terrific, but do you mind if we get another one, just for safety? Maybe try it with a little more . . . *internal* angst?" I asked, with a smile as big as I could muster.

"Sorry, Director Veronica, but once artistic perfection has struck, there isn't more we can do," he explained.

"Just one more . . . ," I pleaded.

"Well, what does everyone think? Did we get the shot, my friends?" Clem asked the other campers, whose immediate calls of "Woo!" and "Yeah!" sealed the deal.

This couldn't happen. I was starting to panic. I needed to get this ending right. I needed to get the ending to be as perfect as I wanted it to be! I needed to use my powers to get Clem to redo the shot my way!

"I'm going to head back to the theater now, my film friends!" Clem announced, flinging the muddy towel back to Nick.

I had to hurry. I closed my eyes tight and tried to focus on an emotion, any emotion that would help Clem stay and reshoot. But my body wasn't cooperating. I was so tired and

drained that I couldn't drum up any real emotion concern-
ing Clem Aldicott other than anger, and even that wasn't
very strong. I did my best to force it, but suddenly I was
really woozy and dizzy. It felt like I was trapped inside an
old-fashioned staticky TV instead of a flat grassy park in the
sun. Trying to steady myself, I put my hand on the small
TV monitor we used to see, in real time, what Betsy was
filming with her camera. When I tried to open my eyes, the
sunlight felt like it was searing my corneas. Something not
good was happening.

"Toodles, everyone!"

I heard Clem's voice get farther away. Time was
running out.

"No!" I said. Simultaneously I felt a series of intense
jolts shoot from my head, down my arms, and out my fingers! I opened my eyes just as I heard a rather ominous
Boom!

The sunlight didn't bother me anymore and I could
finally see again, but I definitely didn't like what I saw.
Smoke billowed out of the TV monitor, Betsy had dropped
the camera and was blowing on her bright-red hand, and
the Tech Twins were smacking on the heads of all the

microphones, trying to make them work. Oh no! My powers had sent an electrical surge through me and into all the equipment! Everything was fried!

"Are—are you okay, Betsy?" I asked, crouching down next to her as she tended to her hand.

"It's fine," she said gruffly. "Not burned, just really, really hot."

"You guys okay?" Charlie called through his monster mask as he jogged up to us.

"Geez, we're fine," Betsy snarled. "The footage, on the other hand, probably isn't."

I felt all the color go out of my face.

"What?! Did I kill the movie?" I whispered frantically to her.

"Of course this was you," she sighed, realizing it was my powers. Then she wrapped her hoodie around her hand to protect it from the still-hot camera and started looking through its digital files. "A power surge like that could've wiped out everything."

"But?" I asked hopefully.

The rest of the campers, Nick, Ellie, and Ted had joined us. They were just as worried as I was.

"But," she continued, "we didn't lose everything."

A collective sigh washed through the group.

"We lost about seventy-five percent," Betsy finished flatly.

Our movie was gone. And it was all my fault.

"How did this even happen?" Nick asked, looking at the dead monitor.

"I—I think it was me," I said without thinking.

In unison, all the campers' heads swiveled around to look at me.

"I, uh . . ." I stumbled, trying to find a reasonable lie. "I *may* have overloaded the power outlet inside by plugging too many things into it."

I gave Charlie a sideways glance. Like the best best friend he is, he slowly started backing out of the group and toward the side door of the theater, following the extension cord back to the outlet so he could fake the scene and make it look like I *had* plugged too many things in.

"That doesn't make any sense," Lizzie said. "We checked the power source before we started filming today."

"I, um, went back in and redid the plugs. Right before we shot," I false confessed. I wasn't even sure why I was determined to take the blame—except that it really was my fault. I guess I wanted everyone to know that.

"What? Why?" Dean hissed.

Everyone was looking at me, different levels of annoyance, anger, and sadness all directed at me.

"Because I'm the director?" was the best I could come up with.

"*Pfft.* Some director you are," Hun Su said. "You're supposed to bring everything together, but instead you just destroyed it."

"I'm sorry," I mumbled.

Ellie chimed in, "Guys, it was an accident, I'm sure."

"It was!" I said. That was the total truth.

"There was no reason for Veronica to be messing with *our* job," Max said. "She's been this way the whole time. Everything has to be her way. She is more dictator than director."

"Yeah, Director Dictator!" Lizzie agreed. "And now two weeks of hard work is down the drain."

I couldn't believe this was happening! I had to stop it. I riffled around in my brain and in my heart for the right emotions to make them stop, to make them see that I was right, but there was nothing there. Or nothing I could dig into to transfer onto them. I was so spent from the day before. I felt like I was almost hollow.

Nick held his hands up, pleading, "Everyone. Everyone. I'm sure we can salvage something. And with a little last-minute hustle today, we can reshoot what we need to. We know what we're doing now; it'll be so much easier."

"Dude's right," Ted chimed in. "Let's all chill our grills."

Charlie returned. By the look on his face, I could tell he had been successful at making it look like I'd royally messed up the plugs.

Nick continued, trying to lighten the mood, "See, Charlie is even still in costume, even though we've been done with monster shots for a full day. Ready to go."

"I just like it." Charlie shrugged.

"No!" Avery suddenly shouted. Then, without speaking, he rounded up the rest of the campers, other than me, Charlie, and Betsy, and they all walked off the set.

"Do you think they're coming back?" I asked.

From the sidewalk, Dean yelled to me, "Direct yourself!"

"I think that's a hard no," Betsy answered.

After they left, the three of us helped Nick and Ellie pack up all the equipment and put away all the costumes from the day, save Hun Su's sword, which she had taken with her. She had grown really fond of that thing. Anyway, to say the mood was somber was the greatest understatement of all time. The rest of us were so sad, Betsy's normally dark and melancholy self seemed rather joyous in comparison. Still, Nick tried.

"Let's just wrap for today, all right?" He forced a grin and bumped into me playfully with his shoulder.

I was so embarrassed by all of it. I had been a crummy director. And Nick knew it. Oh, Nick. What I wouldn't give for him to look at me right now the way he'd looked at me back in the Weatherses' kitchen. I realized I hadn't said anything back to Nick. I could still save a little dignity and say something wise and grown-up about the whole thing.

"I think that you are unbelievably cute," I said.

Alert: Those were completely different words than what I had intended to say.

Nick turned to look at me. He was smiling, but he had a completely puzzled look on his face. "What?"

I needed to play it off.

"I'd kill to be your girlfriend," I continued. I wanted to punch myself in the face. What was going on?! Then I realized something had gone wrong, and my powers had made me speak my exact thoughts! I couldn't control them.

Nick chuckled a little, still obviously perplexed.

I focused really, *really* hard. I needed to fix this. *Say the right words, Veri!*

"You smell really good," came out instead.

This, thank goodness, he perceived as a joke and laughed. He gave my hair a good tousle before walking away.

"Tomorrow we'll figure it out, and it will be fine," Nick was telling Charlie and Betsy when I brought back the last of the props.

"Yeah," Ellie added, "we can always show another movie at the theater instead."

I couldn't bear to think of that, or even answer, considering what was happening with my mouth. I needed to be alone. So when Nick offered me a ride home with him and Charlie, I refused. Charlie offered to walk with me, but he also understood that I needed some space.

At this point, I was hoping someone would shoot me up *into* space so that I'd stop messing everything up.

I decided to take the long walk home, through the parking lot and onto the old brick roads that still exist on the outskirts of downtown. I liked looking at the old houses and imagining the people who lived there years ago. Did any of them have to deal with anything as weird as I did? Before I could get too lost in thought as I set off, something caught my eye.

Oh, heck no! If I had an ounce of emotion left in me, this would be a very bad situation. Ms. Watson was standing next to her Jeep in the parking lot. Not leaning, not checking her phone, just standing. It was textbook Ms. Watson.

"You're not supposed to talk to me," I reminded her.

"I believe your father said that I shouldn't 'see' you," she said, "which technically isn't under my control."

"Really mincing words, there. Are you trying to prove to me how sneaky you are?" I asked.

"No, Veronica. I'm being factual. I don't do sneaky. That's not how my brain works," she replied. "I need to ask you something, but not in public. Please get in the car."

"I don't think so. You don't even know how much trouble I'm in with Dad right now."

"You mean the trouble you're in because of your appointments at the Weatherses' house?" she asked.

"How do you know about that? Did Dad tell you?"

"No, your father and I haven't spoken since he . . . ended things." She looked at her shoes for a second. "Please, get in the car."

I did. I kinda had to, didn't I? If Dad was so upset about the tests, then I really needed to be on top of damage control.

"What do you want?" I asked once we were in and the air-conditioning was turned on full blast.

"Want?" she puzzled.

"Yes, what do you want me to do so you keep your mouth shut about my powers," I explained.

"You seem to be mistaken, McGowan," she said, her brow furrowed. "I don't want anything *from* you. I want to help you."

"I don't understand," I told her. And I really didn't.

She picked at a spot of dirt on the steering wheel for a moment before reaching into the backseat and returning with a wet wipe, which she used to wipe the spot. She then continued to wipe down the entire dashboard.

"I saw Weathers breathe fire the other night. In your backyard after your father went to work," she revealed.

"You were *spying* on us?!" I exclaimed.

"Not spying," she said. "I was monitoring."

"How is that any different?" I asked.

"I don't think I'm making myself clear," she mused. "I was monitoring you and Weathers, yes, but not to collect data."

"Why then?" It made no sense to me.

"Because you are children. And children shouldn't be left alone at night. Something might happen. And if something bad happened to you, I'd feel . . ." She slowed down like she couldn't think of the word.

"Responsible?" I tried to help.

"No," she said with renewed clarity. "Sad."

"Sad?" I repeated quietly. Ms. Watson had emotions?

"Yes," she answered as she shoved the wet wipe into a small, novelty garbage can on the floor of the backseat. She turned back around and did her best to look me in the eye. It was becoming apparent that this was really hard for her.

"I know our relationship got off to a rocky start, but I'd be remiss if I didn't inform you that I have grown fond of you."

I realized my mouth was hanging open and closed it. She took that as a sign to continue.

"Spending time with your father, and as of late, with

both of you, has added a dimension to my life that it had been lacking." She added, "And I am very grateful."

Guilt struck me hard and fast. I noticed my shirt was now striped, like an old-time prison uniform! My powers had started up again, really showing my guilt. Ms. Watson wasn't some spy out to sabotage my powers or even a mean lady who wanted to take my dad away from me. She was lonely, just like me.

"Did your condition just do something?" she asked, pointing to the stripes.

"A little," I confessed. "I'm kinda depleted lately."

"Well, forcing your condition onto others seems like it would be very draining," she agreed.

"Yeah, wait, rewind. How do you know about that?" I had gotten so wrapped up in learning that Ms. Watson was not an evil person that I'd glossed over the part where she knew everything.

"Well," she explained, "I saw Weathers breathe fire but ruled him out completely for having the condition the next day, after I followed you to his home. It didn't take time to put the pieces together. Especially after viewing the changes on your film set since then. This was, in fact, once my job."

"Oh snot," I said, realizing how careless I had really been the past week.

"Oh snot, indeed," she said dryly. "So, when your father ended things so abruptly, especially when he and I had discussed quite an opposite set of events beforehand, I could deduce that you had forced your viewpoint onto him."

I was deep in thought trying to untangle the past few days. I must have been silent for too long.

"That is, unless I am sorely mistaken," Ms. Watson said cautiously.

"Oh no. You're right," I confessed. "I just—I thought—I don't know. Everything is a big flibbin' mess right now."

"I agree," she said.

"I'll tell Dad what I did," I told her. "It was super dumb of me to try to mess you guys up."

"Thank you," she said.

"I wish everything else was that easy to fix," I complained.

"If there is one thing I learned in my years of civil service, it's that everyone's opinion deserves to be respected. You don't have to agree with them, but you also don't have to change their minds. Sometimes letting people make their own decisions is all you can do."

It wasn't bad advice. I just had no clue how to apply it to my own situation.

"I should get going," I said, opening the door. "I'm sorry I've been such a pain."

"That's all right, McGowan."

"You can call me Veronica, you know? If you're going to be around more often, that is."

She looked at me. "I hope I will be."

I shut the door and started heading home. I had a lot of work to do tonight. And that was after I came clean to Dad.

"So, I need to talk to you," I said quietly.

My dad was sitting on a bar stool outside the door of the club, checking IDs. He didn't look up when I spoke to him. He carried on with work.

"That's surprising," he said blandly. "You actually want to tell me things now?"

I deserved that.

"Listen," I said after no more people were lined up to get in, "I'm sorry. I'm really sorry I didn't tell you about the tests."

"I feel a big 'but' coming," he predicted, finally looking at me.

I took a deep breath and let it out. "Worse"—I stumbled—"an 'and.'"

I told him about the power transfer and how I had been kinda using it to make things run smoother for the movie. Then I used it on him to try to keep Ms. Watson out of our lives.

"You brainwashed me?" he asked, white-knuckling the tiny flashlight he used to check ID.

"No!" I said quickly and loudly. "I forced you to see things my way."

"So you brainwashed me. And you brainwashed all your new friends."

It was useless to argue about brainwashing, so I just tried to explain, "But I realized how awful and stupid and horrible that was."

"Oh yeah? How? You got everything you wanted," he grumbled.

I hadn't gotten a single thing I wanted, that was the most painful part.

"Everyone hates me," my voice warbled.

Dad looked at me, empathy flashing in his eyes.

"Everyone hates me and the movie is a mess. I failed," I said, fighting back tears. "And, even worse, I ruined things for you with Ms. Watson. I thought it would make me happier if you weren't together, but it doesn't. Seeing you less happy makes me less happy." I was now pushing back an ugly cry face.

"Veri," Dad soothed, "it was, like, a really stupid thing to do—"

"I know." My voice cracked.

"But you're a kid. You're going to do a lot of stupid things! Your stupid things are just going to be extra stupid because of your condition. Don't be so hard on yourself. That's my job."

"You did just call me stupid a gajillion times." I chuckled.

"The condition is stupid, but you're a normal kid," he said, taking my hand. "Speaking of it, shouldn't an adorable monsoon be hitting us right now or something?"

"Normally, yeah, I think it would be," I answered. "I think I'm just so wiped out."

"That's a bummer," he said. "It would be great if you could brainwash Isabella to forget all that crap you made me say."

"Well, Pops, I may actually have some good news for you," I smiled at him.

Dad was thrilled that Ms. Watson was the one who figured out what I was doing and he was even more thrilled that he still had a chance with her. I think that was the only thing that saved me from total annihilation. However, I had not given Ms. Watson a chance, like I said I would, so that put me in violation of our stinky death promise from last week, which was a big, stinky bummer. I had to do all of Dad's stinkiest laundry for the next month. That meant his socks, his workout gear, and anything a small child puked on at work. Plugging of the nose was not allowed. Neither was complaining. I definitely didn't tell Dad this, but I got off easy.

After being dealt my BO-laced fate, I went home and was surprised to see that I wasn't totally alone. Betsy and Charlie were sitting on my porch.

CHAPTER TWELVE
DIRECTOR'S CUT

"Hey," Charlie said warmly.

"Hey?" I replied, looking at them both. I wasn't really sure why they were here.

"We're here to clean up your mess," Betsy told me. "Even though you messed it all up, it's still our movie. Some of us still care."

"And because we're your friends," Charlie said, more to Betsy than to me.

Betsy rolled her eyes. "Come on, weirdo. I think there might be just enough footage to make a movie. You better have some soda," she grumbled, lifting her camera-filled backpack onto her shoulders.

Charlie and I shared a small, cautious smile as we went inside. Was Betsy really our friend now?

We started looking through all the footage that survived. There were only a few shots from when I was completely in control. There were a zillion takes of Avery falling downhill, and Hun Su giggling her lines away.

"That *was* pretty funny," Charlie said, chuckling as we watched Hun Su point the wrong end of her sword at the monster.

He was right. Looking at all this footage, there were so many things that made me smile or reminded me of how fun the first part of camp really was. That footage was actually really fun and, though it wasn't a scary horror movie, it was something. Something good. When I saw a few clips of the shots I had controlled, it was like the life got sucked out of the movie. What had looked good to me in real life, in that moment, had no soul on the screen. And worse, it made me feel uncomfortable and miss the times we had all worked together, despite not agreeing on anything. And I mean *anything*.

I realized I had turned into a control freak, and that truth stung. I had taken away the voices of my friends and fellow campers so that they couldn't challenge me. So that

I would always be right. And that was wrong. It wasn't like I was some regular kid who acted dumb and their friends had to talk sense into them, I *had actually* brainwashed them.

Ugh.

I couldn't change the past, but I could at least make a movie they had a voice in. One that we had fun making. One that, once they saw it, would show them how sorry I was.

"Dump all the footage I shot using my powers," I instructed Charlie.

He beamed. "Really?"

"What?" Betsy asked.

"Uh, just get rid of everything that's total crap," Charlie clarified for her.

"Except the funny stuff. We should have a blooper reel during the credits," she suggested.

"That's a fantastic idea!" I agreed.

"Honestly, there's enough footage of Avery rolling down that hill to make a full-length movie just of that," she snorted. "It was just so funny. I couldn't stop filming it." Her snort turned to laughter, which infected Charlie and me, too. Suddenly, there the three of us were, laughing uncontrollably.

This was what I wanted to feel when I watched our movie. Like I was having fun with friends.

"When Avery looks straight into the camera"—I gasped for breath between laughs—"it reminds me of those hilariously awful movies we saw during the classic movie screenings."

Then it dawned on me. I bolted up, straight and alert. Maybe, with a little work, I could make this footage into what it really was: something hilariously awful.

Betsy, Charlie, and I were up all night working on editing the movie together. Scratch that. Around 4:00 a.m., Betsy fell asleep on the keyboard and Charlie had been asleep for roughly two hours already. Still, they didn't *need* to help me, so I was super grateful that they had just showed up at all.

In the end, we had put together a really great, definitely tacky, definitely B-movie monster film, like the black-and-white kind you see on TV late at night where there's a cheesy-looking monster and some quirky, memorable characters who die one by one, sometimes in ways that don't really make sense. It was hilariously bad, but in the best way. The only thing missing was Clem's over-the-top reunion with his daughter. How ironic that what caused me to fry all our footage was now the perfect ending for our film. But the footage hadn't survived.

"Hey," Dad whispered from the doorway of the office. "You still at it?"

I smiled at him. "Just finishing up."

"Did you kill those other two or are they just asleep?" He winked and gestured for me to follow him into the kitchen.

"Are things okay?" I asked him as I leaned against the refrigerator. "You only make pancakes when we're celebrating something."

"Your premiere is tonight," he said.

"That's not it," I pressed. I could tell it was something else. "You and Ms. Watson got back together! Already?"

"I called her right after you left. Turns out, she wasn't even as mad at you as I was."

"That's . . . good."

"But that brings me back to what we started talking about the night you went all brain klepto on me."

"Okay . . ."

A groan came from the den, followed by the appearance

of a rumpled boy. Charlie yawned, then perked right up. "Do I smell pancakes?!"

"No," Dad said. "And we need a family moment here."

"Cool," Charlie said, hopping up onto the counter next to the fridge.

Dad opened his mouth to remind Charlie that he isn't in our family, but then he thought better. "Actually, yeah, Chuck, you should hear this, too, since you pretty much live here anyway."

Dad put down his spatula and turned to us. He had a gleam in his eye, but he also seemed really nervous.

"What is it?" I asked.

He rubbed his rough hands on his apron, making sure to get the palms. They must've been sweaty. He *was* nervous.

"I, uh," he stammered. "We, um . . . Man, this is harder than I thought it would be."

He took a deep breath but didn't let it out. Instead he quickly blurted, "Isabella and I are engaged. We're gonna get married."

I looked at Charlie to verify that I had just heard those words. His slack jaw and wide eyes confirmed it.

Charlie gasped, "Who's Isabella?!"

"Ms. Watson!" I told him.

"No!"

Dad ignored Charlie completely and looked intently at yours truly. "So?" he asked gently, wanting to know how I felt.

I felt a lot of things. In the past twenty-four hours my view on Ms. Watson had changed a little, at least.

But maybe my feelings weren't so important here. I mean, I'm glad when my dad is happy. He seemed happier than he had been in a long time, and though the thought of them kissing made me throw up a little in my mouth, I'd happily puke for his happiness, I guess is what I'm saying.

Did I use the word *happy* enough there?

And if I had learned anything in the past few days, it was that you had to let other people make their own decisions.

"It's cool, Dad," I said, and I gave him a huge hug. "I'm so happy for you!"

He hugged me tighter, obviously relieved. "Thanks, baby. You can be happy for you, too—there'll be another female around these parts. You'll have a stepmom!"

I cringed. "Do I have to call her mom?"

He laughed. "Actually, I don't think she'd go for that, either."

"Can *I* call her mom?" Charlie asked, making us all laugh.

Betsy dragged herself out of the office. Her short black hair was sticking out in all directions, and she had marks from the keyboard on her face. "'Sup?"

There was one more piece of the movie puzzle that needed solving. I had to get Clem Aldicott to redo his cameo and splice it back into the movie. Considering how gung ho he had been about doing it in the first place, I wasn't too worried about asking for an encore.

"Absolutely not," Mr. Stephens trilled, blocking my way into the theater. "You are a menace to society. Everything you touch seems to go up in smoke and I'm not risking it." He added, "Plus, Clem is already in character for tonight's performance. You'll throw him off, just like you threw off your little video film."

"It's eleven a.m.," I replied. "The play doesn't start for another eight hours."

"He's a method ac-tor!" Mr. Stephens painfully enunciated each syllable.

"I didn't know that," I confessed. "So, method acting means that you completely immerse yourself in your character twenty-four seven, right? He thinks he's literally Captain Hook right now?"

"Child. He *is* Captain Hook," Mr. Stephens said, adding a dramatic eye roll.

"He didn't do that for our movie," I told him skeptically.

"That's because your film doesn't matter," he pointed out.

I guess getting the reshoot wasn't going to be as easy as I'd hoped. And I needed it. So I was going to have to try to make a deal.

"What do you want?" I asked Mr. Stephens.

"Pardon?"

"To let me talk to Clem and reshoot for ten minutes. What do you want?"

"I *want* you to cancel your little movie tonight," he demanded.

"You know that's impossible. We have people coming."

"I know. And I want them in my theater. That's what I want. I want to have a full house for opening night, and I don't want you to mess it up. Those are my terms," he stated.

A light flicked on inside my brain. I waved my hand above my head to make sure a light bulb hadn't sprung from my powers. Thankfully no, but I still had an idea!

"What if I told you I could meet your terms?" I asked.

"I'm listening," Mr. Stephens said.

Fifteen minutes later, Clem was giving Charlie, Betsy, and me a repeat performance of his lines. Betsy was recording it on her phone. Not the best setup, but the best we could do. Clem delivered his lines, faithful to his original interpretation, despite being "in character" for his *Peter Pan* performance later that night. Turns out the scope of Clem's acting ability wasn't that vast: the only difference between our Lost Father character and Captain Hook was an intense British accent.

"Daughhhteeeeer!"

I was doing my best not to influence Clem's performance. I still thought it was a little over the top even for our silly film, but I had promised myself that I'd keep quiet. It was hard. Really hard. Normally this is where I'd expect a stupidpower to ruin my day. Where was it? Maybe they were still too depleted from before. If they were half as exhausted as I was, that would make total sense.

"Thank you, Clem," I said after he was finished. "That was perfect!"

"All righty, love," he said, "sees you tonight. Arggh!"

I bowed slightly, then handed back his Captain Hook hat. He clicked his heels and went back into the theater.

Charlie scratched his head. "I don't sound like that, do I?"

Betsy and I looked at each other.

"How'd you get Stephens to let Clem shoot with us again?" Betsy asked, without answering Charlie.

"Just edit that into the end, and Charlie and I will take care of the rest," I assured her. "Meet us back here at six!"

"Here? Why?"

"Because we're having a double feature."

CHAPTER THIRTEEN
BACK TO (SHOW) BUSINESS

Okay, so the deal I made with Mr. Stephens was actually good for all of us. With so much footage missing, our movie was now technically a "short" and probably wouldn't seem like much to the folks who came to our premiere. My idea was that we show our film before the play! Then we BOTH would get a full house for our creations! True, it wasn't beating the pants off the stuck-up Mr. Stephens, but it was better than flat-out losing and no one seeing what we'd worked so hard on. Plus, it was probably the only way I could make things up to my fellow campers.

"What should we do first?" Charlie asked as we headed into town. "We need to call everyone who bought tickets for the movie and tell them to go to the theater instead, and we need to round up the campers."

"That's a lot of phone calls," I said. "Almost fifty people."

"If only we knew someone who thrived on monotonous organizational tasks." Charlie made a thoughtful face and stroked an imaginary beard.

"Ms. Watson!" I exclaimed.

"She's gonna be your *mom*. She *has* to help us."

I laughed. "Please don't say that word."

"Mom? Mom, mom, mom, mom," Charlie sang.

At the dental office, Ms. Watson was more than happy to take on the work.

"Oh, thank heavens," she said, visibly relieved. She pushed a *Modern Bride* magazine aside like it was covered in poo. She noticed me noticing her aversion to the magazine.

"Uh, congrats . . . or welcome to the family, I guess!" I said, realizing that I hadn't officially acknowledged her becoming my official stepmom. *Eeep*.

"Thank you. This should be very interesting," she said.

"I guess we have lots to plan," I added, pointing to the magazine.

"I cannot abide a fluffy dress," she admitted.

"Understandable."

Charlie and I left Ms. Watson, content to dial her day away. Now we had to rebuild the bridges that I had accidentally burned down. At least for the first time in a long time, I hadn't *literally* burned anything down.

First up on our I-know-I-fudged-up-please-don't-hate-me-forever tour were the Tech Twins, Dean and Lizzie. They lived in an apartment downtown, not far from the theater. Unfortunately, their response wasn't as forgiving as I had hoped for.

"We recut the movie," I said through the intercom up to their apartment. "You need to come see it. I promise you'll like it." Charlie and I shared a look. We had no idea if they would like it.

"No," Dean and Lizzie said in unison.

"Lizzie, Dean, Charlie here. We all feel bad about what happened at camp, ya know? Veronica has done her best to fix it."

"No," Dean and Lizzie said in unison.

Charlie and I looked at each other again.

"Is this a recording?" I asked.

"No," Dean and Lizzie said in unison.

"Do you want twenty dollars?" Charlie tested them.

"No," Dean and Lizzie said in unison.

"*Gah!* It's a recording." I grumbled.

"They must have heard we were coming. Pretty smart though, right?" Charlie was impressed. "I should have them set me up with one like that for when my moms try to wake me up."

About a block away, we found Hun Su in a hammock sunning herself in her gigantic backyard. She still had her prop sword next to her. She'd grown way too fond of it.

"Are you drunk with power?" Charlie kidded her.

"Excuse you," she said. She didn't look at us, only pointed the plastic blade in our direction.

"Hun Su, we brought you a ticket for tonight," I said. "You probably don't know, but—"

"But you finished the movie and are now showing it before the play?" She finally turned to look at us and lowered her shades. "Everyone knows."

"So, you'll come?" Charlie asked.

"Haven't decided yet. I mean, it is me on a big screen. I should probably be there. But then there's, like, solidarity with my other campers. Unions and stuff," she explained.

"Unions?" Charlie asked, but I waved him off.

"Listen. I know things didn't go the way we wanted them to, but I fixed it," I told her. "I fixed it and you should come see it. Please."

"I said, I'll think about it." She waved the blade wildly at us.

I stuck the ticket under her bottle of soda and pulled Charlie away.

"Maybe it's better if she doesn't show; at least we'll be a lot less likely to have a sword-related accident at the screening," he concluded as we walked down the sidewalk.

201

Next up was Avery. We knew where he probably was, and our going there would kill three birds with one stone. Which, by the way, is a horrible saying. When was it a cool thing to just go around killing birds? Or a point of pride to kill lots all at once? Gross. The past was kinda terrifying. Sorry! Tangent. Back to it.

Since there wasn't any camp today for them, Avery and the other two were probably at Café Blasé playing Magic: The Gathering.

Charlie got very excited when we spotted them in the corner booth. "Maybe they'll let me play!"

"We gotta focus here, Chief," I said. "They've been here since the place opened, slugging down sugar and caffeinated beverages. We have no idea what the situation will be. Actually, that gives me an idea."

I pulled out the last of my allowance and bought a fresh pitcher of soda and a basket of fries.

"I come in peace," I said solemnly, offering the gifts to Avery, Max, and Rashida.

Their shaky hands, bloodshot eyes, and piles of cards told the tale. They were high on the pure joy of gaming. And also copious amounts of caffeine.

"You can't bribe us to come back," Rashida said matter-of-factly before grabbing a fry.

"I know," I said. Crap. I was really hoping I could bribe them back. "It's just a peace offering that accompanies these." I rifled through my bag until I found their tickets to *Peter Pan*.

Avery let out a deep, heavy, angry sigh. He was a master of nonverbal communication.

"Avery's right," Max said, adjusting his daisy-patterned swim cap. "You're trying to make us feel *better* by giving us tickets to our competitor's show?"

"No, no, no," I said. "We finished the movie. We're going to show it before the play. It's gonna be great, right, Charlie?" I turned to my bestie for some backup, but he was in a daze, practically drooling over the Magic cards.

"So you're telling us to go?" Rashida said. "*Directing* us to go?"

"I'm hoping you'll go," I explained. "It was a lot of work. We should have something to show for it."

Avery rolled his eyes so hard I thought they might get stuck looking into the back of his head.

"Yeah, man," Max nodded at him, then turned to me.

"You mean *you* want something to show for it, Director Dictator."

Now I was getting a little peeved.

"Listen, I know we had our differences, but this is for you guys! Please just come!" I said it way too loudly and dropped the tickets on the table. Then I turned around and did my best to calmly stroll out the door, but I'm fairly sure it looked more like a march. Halfway out the door I realized Charlie wasn't beside me. I tiptoed back inside and grabbed him. He was still standing, mouth agape, at the cards.

"Sorry," I grunted as I dragged him away.

"They could have at least come up with a combo name for you," Charlie said as we headed toward home.

"What's that?" I asked.

"I mean," he clarified, "they called you Director Dictator. Wouldn't it have been cleverer if they called you Directator?"

I mulled it over. "Maybe, but 'directator' kind of sounds like it has something to do with potatoes. Like I ship 'taters directly to your house."

"I think we just found our new business," Charlie joked.

"Might be my only option. I don't think this whole director thing is working out so well. They aren't going to come."

"You never know." Charlie paused. "There is one wee thing, and Veri, don't get mad when I tell it to you."

"Dude, I think if you have to say, 'Don't get mad,' it probably is a good sign that I'm gonna get mad."

"Fair point," he said. "It's just . . . I noticed that you didn't apologize to anyone."

"What do you mean? Fixing the movie and making it the way they wanted it—the right way—is my apology." My brain caught up with my words. "But I guess they won't know that unless they come. And they probably won't come because they don't think I'm sorry. Crud."

"We don't know that," Charlie said.

"Should I go back and apologize to everyone?" I wondered.

Charlie shook his head no. "Considering how the first course went, I wouldn't go back for seconds."

By then we were on Pleasant Drive, the street where Charlie and I either meet or split up to go to our own houses, depending on the time of day.

"I'm gonna go take a nap," he said.

"I'm going with you," I told him.

"Remember, I snore."

"No. I need to tell your parents that the tests are over." I sighed.

"Oh. Yeah," Charlie sadly replied.

"Your father is aware that we had no intention of actually experimenting on you, correct?" Dr. Weathers asked.

She leaned against the counter in the lab while Charlie and I sat on the hospital bed.

"You didn't?" I asked.

Lucia wheeled closer to us on her desk chair. "Of course not!" She paused for a moment. "But you would really consider letting someone do that to you, just to keep our Charlie here?"

I shrugged, but then nodded. I was surprised to feel my eyes welling up.

I caught Lucia and Dr. Weathers sharing a look. Lucia cocked her head to the side, as if to say, "See?" Then I swore Dr. Weathers rolled her eyes.

"Okay," she finally said.

"We are going to stay for a while." Lucia nodded to Charlie and me.

I gasped.

"What?!" Charlie jumped off the hospital bed in excitement. "You had a change of heart?"

"We had a change of data," Dr. Weathers told him.

"What do you mean?" I asked.

"The changes that you've experienced since we started observing you have been fascinating, Veri," Lucia explained. "We can take those events and try to find other cases with similar reports. It will be enough for us to research and publish for a little while, at least."

"And I'm hopeful we can bribe your father to let us talk with you more," Dr. Weathers added.

"He likes cigars," I offered.

Dr. Weathers made a note of it.

"So, what do you think? Why are my powers showing up on other people?" I asked.

"We can't hypothesize about your condition, Veronica," Dr. Weathers explained.

"In other words you don't know," I stated. "For all we know, this could all be in my head?"

"Certainly not," Dr. Weathers continued. "You half destroyed our lab and made our son breathe fire. We may not know what's causing this, but we do have some valuable observations."

"*But,*" Lucia interjected, "your emotions, your thoughts, all of what happens in your head is part of this. It's your emotions that bring out these powers. I think we can safely say that."

Dr. Weathers hesitantly nodded in agreement. "But we need more data."

"So, does that mean we're staying?" Charlie asked, trying not to let his excitement get the better of him.

"Yes." Lucia grinned. "We are staying."

"*Ahh!*" Charlie and I screamed with joy.

"Thank you! Thank you!!" I ran and hugged Lucia as hard as I could. Then I attempted to hug Dr. Weathers and she obliged me with a pat on my back. Charlie helped by pulling Lucia over to us and pressing us all together in a massive group hug.

Charlie and I were still smiling like idiots when we left the lab and ran right into Nick and Ellie, who were just sitting down in the living room.

"Hey, guys!" Charlie exclaimed.

I felt my cheeks go warm at the thought of the love confession that had dribbled out of my mouth yesterday. To be safe, I nodded my hellos.

"Guys, Veri fixed everything!" Charlie told them. "You have to hear what she did for our movie!"

I looked at my feet, feigning embarrassment, but in reality, I was too scared to speak. I had no idea what was going to come out of my mouth if I had to talk to Nick.

"And she's humble!" Charlie said after a few moments of my silence.

He went on to tell them about our new B movie and my deal with Mr. Stephens, how Ms. Watson was getting everyone to go to the theater, and our attempts to get the crew back together. By the end, Nick and Ellie were both grinning from ear to ear.

"That's amazing!" Ellie squealed.

"I can't wait to see it!" Nick told us as Charlie and I headed to the door.

Then Nick stopped me.

"You know, Veri, you really are a cool kid," he said. He ruffled my hair before turning back into the house.

And there you have it, folks. I was a cool kid. *Kid.*

Lucia was right—it was all in my head.

Outside Charlie and I said our goodbyes.

"Fingers crossed for tonight," he said.

"And toes," I replied.

CHAPTER FOURTEEN
PICTURE-PERFECT ENDING

I nervously waited outside the theater. It was 6:30, and Betsy hadn't shown up with the edited film! We were supposed to start at seven and our audience was already starting to arrive. There were so many things circling around in my head. Would any of the other campers come? Would anyone like our movie? Did I ruin our movie with my edits? Was this dress really worthy of my first film premiere? (I only knew the answer to that last question, which was an easy no. The dress I wanted was not in the budget after paying for camp. Dad had said something about the importance of money for food. I say, food schmood. Girls have only one first premiere.) Anyway, the thoughts were swirling around so ferociously, and I was getting so nervous, that I felt myself start to spin! I quickly gained speed until I was twirling around uncontrollably! My powers had taken over!

"Nothing to see here!" I called out from inside my speed vortex in case anyone was watching me. "Just love me some spinning!"

Thankfully, I felt powerful hands grip each of my wrists, stopping my perpetual motion. I recognized those hands. I feared them.

"Stop, weirdo," Betsy commanded.

My lower half fought it for a moment, but eventually twisted itself out.

"Thank you," I said as she let me go. "I was getting worried about the movie."

"Yeah, I tried to be here sooner, but I had to wait until my mom got home to take over watching my baby brother."

"You have a brother? I had no idea."

"He's pretty new, but he's really rad," she said. Her eyes lightened for a moment. She really loved him. "But, uh, let's set up. We have a show to put on."

Ellie and Nick had been awesome enough to set up

a projection screen onstage so we could play our movie through Nick's fancy laptop and project it onto a big screen.

"Well, at least we could do this without the Tech Twins," I said to Betsy. I was a little bummed that they had refused to even talk to me.

"Some people aren't as forgiving as I am," Betsy replied in a monotone.

I looked around. People were really streaming in! I saw Lucia and Dr. Weathers finding their seats. Charlie must be here!

"We should get backstage," I said. "I bet Nick, Ellie, and Charlie are back there."

On our way, I spotted Dad and Ms. Watson and gave them a wave and a nervous smile. Dad saw that last piece and waved it away, like he was saying, "It's nothin'! You got this!" Then Ms. Watson gave me a very robotic double thumbs-up.

Betsy saw them over my shoulder. "I don't know what is more unsettling, the thumbs-up themselves or the fact that Ms. Watson seems to be in pain doing them."

Backstage we did indeed find Ellie, Nick, and Charlie. Charlie had dressed for the occasion, sporting a tuxedo on his top half and ripped jeans on his bottom half.

"Very nice!" I complimented him.

"Ladies, looking fierce as usual," Charlie said, and gave us a deep bow.

"It was great that you three did so much to help finish the movie," Nick said.

"Well, I was the one to ruin it," I reminded him.

"You didn't mean to," Ellie said. "I hope you know we never thought you did."

"And finishing what you started—especially when things go really wrong—shows an amazing work ethic," Nick added.

"Which is something you definitely need in the film industry," Ellie told us.

Betsy, Charlie, and I shared excited looks.

"I just wish the others were here," I confessed. "They deserve a great night more than I do."

"The show must go on!" Mr. Stephens's voice blared into our conversation, startling us all. He sauntered into our group, a big smile on his face.

"I'm so glad we got this all worked out," he said to Nick and Ellie.

"Well, the kids are pretty resourceful," Nick answered.

"Yes," he agreed and slowly turned to us. "Your

effort has certainly helped. We have a packed house tonight."

Charlie's eyes went wide. "Sold out?!"

Mr. Stephens nodded. "Yes, and I do believe all of your fellow cinema rats are here."

"They came . . . ," I said quietly. Ellie put her arm around my shoulder and gave me a squeeze. I didn't realize there were tears in my eyes.

Nick shook his head in happy disbelief. "Let's start the show."

We waited in the wings while Nick and Ellie introduced the film and got it rolling. There was no way I was going to go anywhere near that equipment now! I wasn't taking any chances.

Nick tapped the microphone. "Testing? Hey, everyone. Thanks for coming. I'm Nick Weathers and this is Ellie Russo. I know tonight was a quick change of plans for a lot of you, but luckily we live in a really small town." (Audience laughter.) "Some of you know that we had a summer camp these past two weeks for local kids to learn about film production. So, without further ado, I present *The Beast of Rip Cord River!*"

As the lights went down, there was a lot of applause

and a "Whoop!" from a large, loud man I knew well. Ellie now stood on one side of me, Charlie on the other. I linked arms with both of them. Nick mussed Charlie's hair and then patted me on the shoulder. I was too anxious to enjoy it. Then the overly dramatic opening music started and I closed my eyes as a few seconds later, right on time, a wave of laughter poured out of the audience. And they kept laughing. We all looked at each other, relieved and astonished. None of us could move for a long time. It almost felt like if we did, it would break the spell.

Clem Aldicott appeared a few minutes later, nudging my shoulder. "Did I miss it?" He was in full Captain Hook costume, ready to start the play.

I knew he meant *his* scene. "No, you're just about to come on," I told him.

"Beautiful," he said, opening part of the curtain to the side so that we could all see the screen, but the audience couldn't see us. Then he used the top of my head as an armrest. "Director Veronica, our time has come."

Betsy peeked around the curtain to get a look at the audience. "They *are* laughing when they are supposed to," she whispered. Then she turned around, her eyes were wide. "Hey."

The rest of us turned to see that Avery, the Tech Twins, Hun Su, Max, and Rashida, all looking a twinge timid, were standing behind us. Ted had wrangled them and brought them backstage.

"Happy family together again!" Ted whispered loudly.

Mr. Stephens hushed him violently.

I smiled at them and gave a little wave before I motioned for them to come over. They did, and before we knew it, we were all linking arms and had formed a circle, just as onscreen Clem belted out, "Daaaaauuughterrrrrr!"

Then it was over. There was a moment of silence that felt like an hour, but then everyone started clapping like crazy! A few whistles, and, of course, many a large, loud "Whoop!" It went on through the hilarious blooper reel that Betsy had made of all of our mistakes.

"Well, get out there!" Clem pushed us, trying to herd us onstage during Avery's last tumble down the hill on the blooper reel.

"It's not a play," I reminded him.

"You take a thankful audience wherever you can get it, kid," he told me.

I looked at Nick and Ellie for guidance.

"I think you guys should definitely take a bow," Ellie said.

"Yeah," Nick agreed. "It isn't often you get to see a movie with the filmmakers in the house."

"Yes!" Clem exclaimed, leading the way.

I watched everyone follow him out. The crowd went wild.

"Go on," Nick said.

A big part of me really felt like I didn't deserve this. If I hadn't ruined everything, I couldn't have fixed everything. Those guys on the stage were the ones who endured. Ellie must have sensed my angst.

"In the end, you brought them all together, Veronica," she said with a gentle smile. "And you brought the film together. Go." She playfully kicked me right in the butt.

I walked onstage, hoping to not be too noticeable. But by then Clem had commandeered a microphone.

"Director Veronica!" he said to the crowd, who were already on their feet. The rest of the campers were clapping and hooting, too. It all felt really surreal!

"I know she would love to say something to all of you," Clem declared, handing me the microphone.

And then I died. Right there.

Okay, I didn't actually die. I was just absolutely dumbstruck and holding the microphone, but I *wanted* to disappear forever. I felt my stupidpowers starting to push through. What was I going to do? I couldn't literally disappear in front of all these people! Scanning the room, I spotted Charlie, who smiled at me encouragingly. He knew this was my absolute nightmare. Instantly I felt a little better. More relaxed. My stupidpowers settled down. Phew!

"Hello, everyone," I said, shocked by how loud my voice was. "Thank you for coming to our movie. Um. It wasn't easy to make a movie in two weeks." I looked at the campers, who were all listening intently. This was my chance. "I'm sure a big part of that was because it wasn't easy making a movie *with me* in two weeks. These guys worked really hard and put up with a lot. If you liked this movie it was because of them, not because of me. I just stitched together all of their best parts, like I was Dr. Frankenstein and they were the monster." I saw Avery blush and it made me even more nervous. "Did you know that the monster isn't called Frankenstein? It's the last name of the doctor who created him. People always think that's the monster's name . . ." I took a breath, realizing I had gone way off topic. "What I'm trying to say is that they were the heart of it. They made this movie be what it was supposed to be, and I thank them so, so much for working so hard, for being so creative, and especially for forgiving me when I didn't even say 'I'm sorry.' I really am sorry." I finally ended my wandering speech, looking at the faces of my friends. They were all smiling. It filled my heart.

The excitement from the movie, the happiness of having made peace with everyone, and the fact that I wasn't struggling to control any of them felt wonderful. Suddenly the magic of the moment overcame me, and the air above all our heads started to sparkle and shine, like it was filled with glitter. I instantly knew it was one of my powers, but everyone else seemed to think it was a great special effect! They oohed and aahed from their seats. Except for my dad, who was finally silent. He *may* have been cringing. Whatever. It was absolutely gorgeous and made the whole theater come alive with the magic I felt.

The movie wasn't perfect. We weren't perfect. Scratch that. I'm not perfect. And if I'm honest with myself, I know I never will be. I don't know if any one person could be. We're all a bit of a mess, especially me. Sometimes literally me. And maybe that's part of it. The movie was a mess when

I was trying to do it alone, but now it felt perfect. I had been so stressed about what would happen, but then it became magical and perfect once I opened up to it. My powers are a mess, but occasionally they can do beautiful things when I let good emotions fill me. Maybe we need the mess to make perfection.

Or maybe the mess *is* perfection.

EPILOGUE

So, there you have it. Another slightly outrageous series of events. If I was old enough to gamble, I'd put all my money on this not being the last weird thing that happens to me. Even though my power transfer seems to have worn off, and I've promised Dad to never ever, ever, ever, ever, ever, ever let anyone experiment on me (an endless stinky death would await me), I'm still not just your average kid. Will I ever be? That's hard to say. But truthfully, I have bigger things to worry about right now. First thing: School starts in a week! How is it that the school year drags on and on, but summer vacation seems to be done before you even get the hang of wearing flip-flops? A new year means a fresh start, and since I'd obliterated everyone's memory of my powers at the end of last year, I really could start fresh! I wasn't sure what that meant yet, but that was okay. I'd have Charlie by my side. (Phew!) And Betsy? We were friends now? Is it friendship if it always has a question mark after it? Time will tell. Or she'll kill me in my sleep. Either is fair game at this moment.

Thing two: Dad and Ms. Watson have set a wedding date. It's soon. Like, in two months soon. Naturally, I've been plunged deep into wedding planning. And, whether I liked it or not, that was what I was doing with every spare moment I had. Including this one.

"This is ludicrous," Ms. Watson said as she turned around on the carpeted pedestal. The white gown more or less engulfed her. I couldn't help but giggle.

"Sorry," I said.

"You have every right to laugh, Veronica McGowan."

She hadn't quite gotten to just calling me Veronica yet. We were working on it, though. Speaking of which . . .

"Maybe you should try on something simple"—I braced myself—"Isabella."

She gave me a reassuring look. "Please, Veronica McGowan, call me Watson."

That I could do.

She continued, "And I have a far more logical idea. Let's get out of here."

"I couldn't agree more." I grabbed my bag.

"Where to?" she asked after we said our goodbye to the sales associate. "Your father doesn't expect us back for hours."

"The movies?" I suggested hopefully.

"What's playing?" she asked.

"I dunno," I replied. "It'll be an adventure."

Watson opened the door for me. "With you, it always seems to be."

Acknowledgments

A huge thanks to the team at Imprint, especially Erin Stein and John Morgan for their support and confidence in our books.

Bernadette Baker-Baughman, you have been instrumental in making my dream job a reality. Thank you for looking out for me in so many ways.

Simini Blocker, your art never ceases to amaze. Thank you for bringing so much life to this series.

To my biggest supporter, Paul Morrissey. Your belief in me keeps me afloat.

Thanks to my family: Mom & Dad; Ryan, Crystal & Logan; and Jeremy, Rhonda & Seamus for being so understanding of my weird schedule and for always being excited about what I'm working on.

To my ladies, Katie Strickland, Natasha Levinger, and Katie Mack, thank you for reminding me how wonderful and life-giving true friendship can be.

About the Author

Heather Nuhfer was born near the Allegheny Mountains where, from the safety of her bedroom, she wrote stories featuring her own monsters.

While working at the Jim Henson Company, Heather finally met many creatures face-to-face, including the lovable characters of Fraggle Rock. Heather scripted the lead story in Henson's Harvey Award–nominated Fraggle Rock graphic novel series, and she is the author of several My Little Pony: Friendship Is Magic graphic novels. She's also penned stories for *Wonder Woman, Teen Titans GO!, The Simpsons, Scooby Doo,* and *Monster High,* and her episodes of Hasbro's *Littlest Pet Shop* are set to air in 2018. *My So-Called Superpowers* is her first prose novel.

When she isn't writing, Heather loves to knit while watching bad 1990s action movies with her beloved furbaby, Einstein.